HEAT
OF THE
MOMENT

ALSO BY LAUREN BARNHOLDT

HEAT
OF THE
MOMENT

THE MOMENT OF TRUTH BOOK 1

LAUREN BARNHOLDT

An Imprint of HarperCollinsPublishers

HarperTeen is an imprint of HarperCollins Publishers.

Library of Congress Cataloging-in-Publication Data
Barnholdt, Lauren, author.
Heat of the moment / Lauren Barnholdt. — First edition.
        pages   cm. — (A moment of truth ; Book 1)
Summary: "Before graduation, I promise to learn to trust" is what the email Lyla McAfee wrote to herself as a freshman, to be delivered right before graduation, says—but on the senior trip to Florida she discovers that what she now considers a silly sentiment may be a lot harder, and a lot more important, than she thinks.
ISBN 978-0-06-232139-8 (pbk.)
1. High school students—Juvenile fiction.   2. Electronic mail messages—Juvenile fiction.   3. Trust—Juvenile fiction.   4. Dating (Social customs)—Juvenile fiction.   5. Best friends—Juvenile fiction. [1. Trust—Fiction.   2. Dating (Social customs)—Fiction.   3. Best friends—Fiction.   4. Friendship—Fiction.   5. Email—Fiction.]   I. Title.
PZ7.B2667He   2015   2014030712
813.6—dc23   CIP
[Fic]   AC

Typography by Ellice M. Lee
15 16 17 18 19   CG/RRDH   10 9 8 7 6 5 4 3 2 1

First Edition

ONE

Before graduation, I will . . . *learn to trust.*

I forgot about that stupid email a week after I sent it, and honestly, I haven't thought about it since. I mean, who even writes something like that? Before graduation, I will learn to trust? That is the most ridiculous thing I've ever heard in my life.

Why didn't I write something a little more . . . I don't know, succinct? You know, something a little more . . . definitive. Like, before graduation I'll go skydiving. Or before graduation I'll lose my virginity. Not that losing your virginity is something you should do just to get it over with. It's not like flossing your teeth or getting a school physical.

Although.

Now that I'm thinking about it, maybe I *should* have written that. I mean, I was only fourteen and a freshman when Quinn, Aven, and I wrote those emails to ourselves and scheduled them to be sent right before our high school graduation. The three of us were in a very sort of emo phase back then. So we went to the beach and started a bonfire and got all morose and spiritual and decided to each write one thing we wanted to accomplish before graduation.

Looking back, the whole thing seems ludicrous.

Of course I know how to trust.

I definitely should have written about losing my virginity.

I mean, it would make sense, since that's the one I'm going to be working on this weekend.

I stare at the email that's appeared on the screen of my phone and then shove it back into my bag. I have bigger things to think about than some dumb email I sent four years ago. Mainly, the fact that I'm late. (Not *that* kind of late. Have to have sex for that to happen, ha-ha.) Late for my senior trip to Florida. Actually, late for the bus that's supposed to take my class to the airport.

It's extremely upsetting. A, because I'm never late to anything; B, because this trip is super important to me (see the aforementioned hint about losing my virginity); and C, because if I miss the flight, there's, like, no way to take a later one.

It said it right on the informational packet they sent out: "ANY STUDENT MISSING THE FLIGHT WILL NOT BE ALLOWED TO MEET UP WITH THE GROUP LATER AND WILL NOT BE REFUNDED THEIR TRIP FEE."

Lots of times they do things like that just for a scare tactic, but I was pretty sure they meant it this time. They already had almost two hundred kids going to Florida—they didn't need to be saddled with additional flights and people showing up late.

"Can't you go a little bit faster?" I ask my mom, shifting in the passenger seat of her Jeep.

She's driving me crazy. No pun intended.

"I'm going the speed limit," my mom says, raising her hand slightly to check the speedometer. Obviously she doesn't get that the speed limit isn't really the top limit of how fast you can go. You can go five miles over without having to worry about being pulled over. It's, like, a fact.

"If I don't make the bus, I can't make the flight," I say. The paper was very clear about that, too. You can't just show up at the airport by yourself and expect to meet up with everyone. You need to ride the bus over. It's some kind of liability thing. "And if I don't make the flight, then I can't get my money back. None of it. Not even, like, a percentage."

She frowns and looks down at the speedometer again. A second later, the needle moves so she's going two miles over the speed limit. I sigh. My mom has always been kind of . . . scattered. Like this morning, for example. It took her fifteen minutes to make one cup of coffee—she kept getting distracted by all kinds of ridiculous things. And then when we got into the car, she took out her wallet and started pulling out pictures of me and babbling about how she couldn't believe her baby was going on a senior trip to Florida, and didn't time fly and she remembered my first day of school and how scared I was and blah blah blah. (Who keeps pictures in their wallet anymore, anyway? She definitely might have ADHD. Like, for sure. She's been reading tons of self-help books lately about taking control of your life—*The Five-Minute Manager! Take Control of Your Time! You Are Not Your Distractions!*—but I'm starting to think she might be better off with an Adderall prescription.)

I watch as the digital clock in the car inches forward.

6:58. 6:59. We're supposed to be there by seven o'clock. At 7:02 we hit a red light so long I have to bite my lip to keep from screaming.

When we finally pull into the school parking lot, there's no bus.

The bus is gone.

"The bus is gone!" I screech.

I pull my phone out and look for a text from Derrick. Derrick is my boyfriend. The one I'll be losing my virginity to this weekend. He would have texted me if the bus was about to leave. He's very good about things like that. But there's nothing. No text. No warning.

Is it possible I have the time wrong? Maybe the bus is going to leave at eight, and I'm actually an hour early! I ruffle through the informational packet I brought with me, but it says "SEVEN A.M." in big capital letters. Great. Just great. Am I going to miss the trip? I can't miss the trip. This trip is important! I've been looking forward to it all year.

My mom, obviously in denial, keeps driving toward the school. She definitely doesn't get it yet. As the car gets closer to the front circle, I see someone standing on the sidewalk, right where the bus should be. Derrick! He probably waited for me! He probably decided that if I wasn't going to Florida, then he wasn't going either. I wonder if he had some sixth sense about me losing my virginity to him this weekend. (I swear he saw an article up on my phone about whether it's supposed to hurt. Talk about embarrassing.) And that's the only reason he even wanted to go on this trip. The thought is both despicable and thrilling at the same time.

I feel flushed. My whole body is on fire thinking about it. Of course, now we're not going to be going on the trip because we've missed the bus. But perhaps it's for the best. Maybe I can convince my mom that we're going anyway, and then Derrick and I can get a room somewhere and spend the weekend just . . . doing it. I heard it gets better the more you do it, and there's no way we'd be able to have a lot of sex in Florida. There are going to be teachers everywhere. And sex is one of the things they're definitely going to be on the lookout for. That and inappropriate swimwear. It was all over the informational packet, a bunch of warnings about inappropriate swimwear. I don't know why they think inappropriate bathing suits are going to be the thing that leads to our demise. All the bathing suits I packed are extremely appropriate (well—except one), and all I can think about is how—

Oh.

Wait.

That's not Derrick.

The guy standing by the traffic circle. It's not Derrick.

"Where's the bus?" my mom asks as she stops the car, like I hadn't just told her it was gone. She does that sometimes— tunes me out when she's distracted and/or thinks I'm being dramatic.

"Obviously gone," I huff. I'm texting Derrick now, try- ing to figure out how far away the bus has gotten. Maybe I can catch up with it somewhere. Like if it stops at a red light or something, I can just run up to it and get on. Of course, that will be horribly embarrassing. Probably everyone will be looking.

Where r u? I type. *I missed the bus.*

I hit send at the exact moment someone knocks on my window.

I scream and drop my phone.

It's Beckett Cross. He must have been the one standing on the sidewalk.

He gives me a smile and then motions for me to roll down the window.

"Hi," he says.

"Hi." I don't know Beckett. He's been in a few of my classes, but he doesn't really say much. But in sort of a cool way. Like, he's not quiet or insecure or anything like that. He's also not really in the popular crowd, although he has some popular friends.

"We missed the bus," he says. His voice is cool, calm, like he couldn't care less about missing the trip. Probably he doesn't. Why would he? He's not the one who's made the decision to lose his virginity. I'm sure Beckett's virginity is long gone, and any sex he was going to have on this trip can be replaced locally with whatever random underclassmen are always following him around the halls like lovesick puppies. Not that I blame them. Beckett is very good-looking.

"I know," I say. "Do you know how long ago it left?"

"No." He shrugs. Obviously he doesn't realize how important this trip is.

"That's okay," I say nonchalantly. "There's a late bus." The lie is out of my mouth before I realize what I'm even saying. There is no late bus. I don't even know why I'm saying it.

"A late bus?" Beckett frowns.

"Yeah. It should be here in about ten minutes. It's just, you know, a stopgap in case anyone misses the bus."

My mom sighs loudly. "Lyla, why didn't you tell me there was a late bus? I was speeding to get here."

I resist the urge to roll my eyes. I can't be spending too much energy on my mom's delusional idea that she was speeding when she so obviously wasn't. I have bigger problems, i.e., figuring out how I'm going to get to the airport so I can go on this trip.

Beckett stoops down and leans in so that he can see my mom. "Hello," he says amicably. "I'm Beckett."

"Hello," my mom says. "I'm sorry we missed the bus."

"No problem," Beckett says, like he's a teacher who's in charge of everything instead of just another student who's in the same situation as I am. He shoots my mom a smile, then straightens up and opens my door for me, like he's a chauffeur. I'm not sure what to do, so I just get out.

He's standing on the curb, and he doesn't step back or anything, so I have no choice but to step up onto the curb next to him. My back is against the car, and I'm so close I can see the chocolate-brown specks in his green eyes. It feels weird being this close to someone other than Derrick. The side of Beckett's mouth turns up into a grin, almost like he can sense my discomfort. I wait for him to move and let me pass, but he doesn't. He just stands there, like he owns the sidewalk.

He smells like strawberry gum and spicy aftershave. I flush and maneuver around him toward the back of the car, where I wait for my mom to hit the release button for the back door. I pull out my carry-on. It's one of those rolling ones, and it's packed to the brim with stuff. Fortunately, the bags we were checking had to be left at the school yesterday, so they could load them all onto the bus. They didn't want to waste time doing it this morning. At the time I thought it was a huge pain in the ass, but now I'm thankful. If I can somehow get to Florida, at least my suitcase will be there.

"All right, well, see you later," my mom calls out her window.

"You're leaving?" The thought is suddenly panic-inducing. What the hell am I thinking, lying about there being a late bus? How am I going to get to the airport? And besides, I don't want to be left here alone with Beckett. I don't even know him. He's one of those people who you never know what they're going to do or say. He's unpredictable. I don't like things that are unpredictable. Which is obviously why I've *planned* to lose my virginity.

"I have to get to work," my mom says. "Text me when you get on the bus."

"We'll be fine," Beckett says. "I'll make sure she texts you, don't worry."

My mom smiles at him, like Beckett's in charge of her

life or something and not just some kid she met, like, five minutes ago.

"Bye, Lyla!" she calls. She blows me a kiss out the window. And then she's gone.

Beckett picks up my carry-on and starts wheeling it back over toward the traffic circle. "Wow," he says. "This is heavy."

"It's not that heavy," I say, rolling my eyes.

He gives me a weird look and keeps walking. He has long legs, and his strides are long on top of it. He's wearing baggy jeans, a crisp white T-shirt, and clean black sneakers. His hair is disheveled in that I-don't-care-what-my-hair-looks-like-but-I-still-look-sexy kind of way. Not that I think Beckett's sexy. I mean, yes, abstractly I can tell he's good-looking. But I have a boyfriend.

"What do you have in here, anyway?" he asks, like he really wants to know.

"Just the normal stuff." Makeup, a couple of dresses, a book, my inappropriate bathing suit (just in case they decided to go through the bags we were checking—they said they weren't, but who knows? There's really no privacy when it comes to schools.).

Beckett looks at me out of the corner of his eye, like he thinks I'm up to something. What could I be up to with a suitcase? Maybe he thinks I'm a drug smuggler.

"I can wheel my own suitcase," I say.

He ignores me and just keeps walking back toward the

front of the school, where he was standing when we first pulled in.

There's a small black duffel bag sitting on the curb, and he sets my bag down gently next to his. He looks at my bag, like he's trying to figure out a puzzle. He reaches out and grabs the tag with my name and address on it, running his finger over the pink marker I used to print the information.

"You like pink," he says, like there's something wrong with it.

"It was the only pen I had." It's a lie. I love pink. But something is making me feel like I have to defend my color choice to him, which is ridiculous. I hardly know him. This is why high school is completely messed up and misogynistic. If it were two guys out here, would Beckett really be commenting on the color of the ink on my name tag? Well, maybe. If it were pink, he might say something.

But whatever. The point is that if it were a guy, I wouldn't have felt the need to defend myself and lie about my choices. I should just tell him I like pink. There's nothing *wrong* with liking the color pink. It doesn't mean anything. I'm a very strong woman. I have a 4.0 GPA, I take three AP classes (which Beckett should know, since he's in two of them), and I'm going to Cornell in the fall. With Derrick. We're both going to Cornell. Isn't that so perfect?

"So," I say, "um, well, thank you for doing that." The new plan is to get rid of Beckett, then call a cab and have them bring me to the airport. I pull my phone out and google "cheap cabs last minute." I know even a cheap cab is going to be ridiculously expensive. But that's what I have a credit card for. I got it a few months ago after getting an offer in the mail. My mom totally flipped and said that I was playing with my financial future. But if I don't use the credit card for the cab, then I'm playing with my sexual future. And that seems far more dangerous.

"You're welcome." Beckett glances at his watch. "So what time does this late bus come, anyway?"

I don't know why, but I'm nervous about telling him there's no bus. Oh, well. It's like pulling off a Band-Aid. Just have to get it over with. "There is no bus," I say cheerfully.

"What do you mean?" He looks puzzled.

"I mean there is no late bus."

He's still perplexed. "What do you mean there is no late bus?"

"I mean that we missed the first bus. And there is no late bus." For someone in AP classes, he's having a really hard time with comprehension.

"Then why did you say there was?" he asks slowly. He's looking at me like I might be totally crazy.

Humph. He wouldn't be looking at me that way if he knew the truth. That I've been planning this weekend for months, ever since my friend Juliana and I had a talk about it and I realized I was ready. But obviously I couldn't just, you know, have sex with Derrick right away. I needed it to be special. And what's more special than a senior trip to Florida?

"Hello?" Beckett asks.

"Oh. Um, well, I just . . . Look, the truth is I really want to go. But obviously my mom wasn't going to let me unless she thought I was going to get there safely."

He's gaping at me. "So you made up a fake late bus?"

I nod. Wow. There really are not that many cab companies around that promise to come at a moment's notice. Most of them say "please allow sixty minutes for pickup." Sixty minutes? What is this, pizza delivery? Sixty minutes is not going to get me to the airport on time.

"And what about me?" Beckett turns my suitcase on its side and sits down on it. The material sags under his weight.

"What do you mean?"

"I mean, did you even stop to think that it wasn't very nice to get my hopes up over some fake late bus? I was just about to leave when you pulled up."

Oh. Yeah, I never thought of that. "Are you upset?"

He grins. "Not really." He fiddles with the thin silver chain he's wearing around his neck. "I think it's kind of awesome. What's your name anyway?"

I stare at him incredulously. "You're kidding, right?"

"Pink?" he tries.

"Pink?"

"Yeah." He grins in that maddening way of his and then fingers the tag on my bag again. "'Cause you write in pink. Not that you look anything like her. Pink, I mean."

I'm not sure if he means it in a bad way. That I don't look like Pink. Does he think Pink's attractive and I'm not? Or is he just stating it as a fact, like "you don't have blond hair" or something?

"I cannot believe you don't know my name," I say. "We're in two of the same classes." I'm still scrolling on my phone, and I've found the number for "Kwiki Cab." Hmm. They promise to pick you up in ten minutes or less. I'm a little worried about their lack of proper spelling, but beggars can't be choosers. And I'm sure it's fine. Companies are always trying to find ways to get you to remember them. Like this time I saw a dump truck that said LET US FILL YOUR HOLE. Totally inappropriate. And yet I still remember them.

I hit call, but Beckett reaches out and grabs my phone.

"Hey!" I grab for it, but he holds it out of my reach and ends the call. "What the hell are you *doing?*"

"What are you going to do, call a cab?"

"Yes!"

"And then what?"

"What do you mean and then what?" My heart is starting to pound now, and I'm getting really anxious, like my whole body is a rubber band that's being pulled tight and ready to spring. Every second that goes by, that bus is getting farther away. Every second that goes by, the plane is getting closer to taking off and leaving me here. All alone. By myself. Virginity intact.

"And what is a cab going to do? Come and take you to the airport? You heard what the school said. That you have to be on the bus, otherwise it's a liability."

"That's obviously a lie," I say. "Of course they're going to let me on the plane." I take my phone from his hand, and this time, he just lets me grab it. This is deeply unsatisfying. I wanted him to hold it out of my reach again, so I could wrestle him to the ground, and then when I finally got my phone back it would feel like some kind of real victory.

I dial Kwiki Cab.

It rings.

Once.

Twice.

Three times.

Four times.

"Thank you for calling Kwiki Cab. . . . We are not accepting new rides at this time, as all our cabs are helping existing customers. . . ."

What? So early in the morning? God, it's probably all drunk people on their walk of shame. How annoying. I try again, but it's the same thing.

I hang up and dial Derrick. It doesn't even ring before I get the greeting telling me to leave a message. I take in a bunch of short, deep breaths through my nose. But the tightness around my chest is making it hard to exhale, so I hold the air in my lungs until they start to burn. I don't want to stay here. I *can't* stay here. My eyes well up with tears.

"Hey, hey, hey," Beckett says, running his hand through his hair and looking uncomfortable. "Please don't cry. Jesus, if there's one thing I can't stand, it's when chicks cry."

"I'm sorry, I just . . . I really wanted to go on this trip." I sniff, and he reaches into his pocket and hands me a Kleenex.

I look at it suspiciously.

He rolls his eyes. "It's clean."

"Thanks." I'm suddenly embarrassed. I blow my nose and then throw the tissue into a trash can. "I'm just . . . I need to be alone for a minute." I pick up my suitcase and start rolling it away from him, down toward the football field where the bleachers are. I just need to think of a plan. But what plan? All my friends are on the bus, going to the airport. And there's no way I can call my mom.

It takes me a second to realize Beckett's following me.

"Okay, fine," he says, sounding exasperated, like I've been asking him questions this whole time. "I'll take you."

"You'll take me?"

"To the airport."

I stop. "How?"

"How what? I have a vehicle."

"You have a *car*? And you've been sitting here this whole

time waiting?" What is wrong with him? Doesn't he know the plane is going to take off any minute, leaving him here, alone and cold in the stupid drizzly Connecticut weather instead of on the warm and sunny beaches of Florida?

He shrugs. "I was trying to decide if this trip was worth the effort of driving all the way to the airport."

"But now you're going to drive us?" My heart is leaping and jumping! I'm excited. I'm freaking out. It's too good to be true!

"Yes. I'm going to drive us. Well, you. I don't think I'm going to go after all." He waves his hand in the air like he can't believe he even was thinking about going on such a lame trip in the first place.

"But you just said that we weren't going to be able to get on the plane. You know, because of liability." I hiccup.

"No one will know you weren't on the bus," he says confidently. "They won't be able to prove it. Just get one of your friends to vouch for you, and make them think they didn't check you off." He shrugs with the nonchalance of a guy who's used to getting his way.

"How do you know?" I ask.

"Trust me." He says it the exact same way someone who should never be trusted would say it.

I hesitate. My heart is telling me to go with him. My mind is saying he's a strange boy, that I know nothing about him, that he could be an ax murderer, that it's borderline inappropriate to get into a car with a guy who isn't my boy-friend. But honestly, what other choice do I have? If I want to go on this trip, I have to get to the airport. It's, like, a law of physics.

And that's when my phone buzzes.

I pull it out, expecting it to be Derrick. But it's not.

One new email.

I pull it up.

To: Lyla McAfee (lyla.mcafee@brightonhillshigh.edu)

From: Lyla McAfee (lyla.mcafee@brightonhillshigh.edu)

At first I'm confused. Why would I be sending an email to myself? It must be one of those phishing scams, the kind that are from some fake email address and make you enter in all your personal information so they can steal all your money. Not that I have any money.

I go to delete it.

And then I remember. The beach. The bonfire. The sand in my toes and the way my face felt tight from my sunburn. Aven and Quinn, laughing, our hair whipping into our faces from the wind. Setting the email to be delivered multiple times so we wouldn't be able to just ignore it.

Before graduation, I will . . . *learn to trust*.

I know it doesn't mean anything. Just because this email is showing up again right after Beckett told me to trust him doesn't mean that I should. The email is stupid. I should have made a promise to lose my virginity.

Of course, if I'm going to have any chance of doing that this weekend, I need to get to Florida. And in order to get to Florida, I'm going to have to get to the airport. And in order to get to the airport . . .

"Okay," I say, sighing. "Let's go."

TWO

IT'S A MOTORCYCLE.

Beckett drives a motorcycle.

"You drive a motorcycle," I say. My voice doesn't even sound shocked. Probably because it's not all that shocking. What would be shocking is if Beckett drove something normal and reliable, like a Nissan Sentra or a Honda Accord.

"Yes, I drive a motorcycle. Well, sometimes. It's not mine." He opens the back compartment and starts rummaging around inside it. He doesn't elaborate on whose motorcycle it is or how he came to be driving it. "I know there's an extra helmet back here somewhere," he mumbles.

I start to feel a little light-headed. I'm not the kind of girl who likes to do things like ride fast in cars or go on Ferris wheels. I get motion sickness.

He pulls out a small black helmet and looks at it. "No cracks," he says happily before handing it to me.

A vision of me on the highway with my brains splattered all over flies through my head. "What are we going to do with my bag?" I ask, motioning to my carry-on.

"We'll put it under the seat."

He picks it up and puts it in, shuts the compartment, and then slings his leg over the motorcycle seat. I try not to stare at the way his legs look straddling that thing. I never thought I was into the whole boy-on-a-motorcycle look (Derrick drives a Nissan Sentra, or his mom's Toyota RAV4 whenever she lets him), but I have to admit Beckett looks good on his bike.

"Be careful with my bag," I say irritably. "It has all my stuff in it."

"Everyone is so obsessed with material things these days. Stripped down is what we should be striving for, don't you think?"

Obviously not. I packed enough for three weeks when we're only going away for four days. But I don't want to seem like I'm a baby or anything, so I just say, "I need my clothes." My voice sounds slightly . . . strangled.

He turns the ignition and the bike roars to life. "So what do you say?" he asks, grinning at me. "Are you in or are you out?"

"Can't we just try to find a cab?" I ask desperately. There have to be other companies. Or maybe a car service! My cousin lives in New York City, and she's always calling car services. They must have them here, too. You know, for, like, businessmen. If I could pick a superpower, that's what I'd pick. The ability to make cabs appear out of nowhere.

Beckett shakes his head. "You already tried that. It will take forever."

"We could try again," I say lamely. "Even if it takes forever, that doesn't mean we're going to miss the flight." The bus was going to get there extra early anyway, because we had so many people. Kind of like how when you go to a restaurant and you have a big party, you have to call ahead so they can make sure they can accommodate you.

"No, Pink." He revs the engine and then raises his eyebrows. "Are you in or are you out?"

I sigh.

"I'm in."

By the time we get to the airport, I feel like I'm going to throw up and my thighs hurt from squeezing them around the bike so hard. Beckett was actually driving surprisingly slow, but I didn't like the feeling of being so . . . exposed. Every time we would take a turn, all I could think about was my poor little bones bouncing all over the highway.

So I held on as hard as I could, figuring if I could at least stay upright, I might be okay even if we crashed. Of course, that also meant I was holding on to Beckett as hard as I could, which was kind of awkward. The wind pushed my cheeks into the back of the T-shirt he was wearing. His laundry detergent smelled like spring, and his back was very, um, muscular.

When we finally get to the airport, Beckett drives right up to the drop-off lane. He cuts the engine, gets off the bike, and pulls off his helmet. He cocks one eyebrow at me, then holds his hand out to help me off the bike.

"Good ride," I say nonchalantly. My knees are a little wobbly, and I take a stutter step backward, knocking against the motorcycle seat.

"Whoa, Pink," Beckett says, sliding his arm around my waist. "I think you need to sit down." He walks me over to one of the benches near the doors.

"I'm fine," I say as I sit down. Pavement. Keeps. Spinning.

He shakes his head. "You should have told me you get motion sickness."

"I don't get motion sickness." Lie, lie, lie.

"Uh-huh." He sits down next to me. "Lean your head down."

"What?"

"Put your head between your legs. You'll feel better, trust me."

I do what he says, mostly because I'm afraid that if I don't, I might end up puking all over him. Or the concrete. Neither of which would be a good idea.

He gathers my hair and holds it up off my neck. The cool morning breeze moves over my skin. "Take deep breaths," he instructs.

I breathe in and out as slowly as I can. Almost instantly I start to feel better.

"Feel better?" Beckett breathes into my ear.

Goose bumps break out on my arms, and the hair on the back of my neck stands up. My heart beats fast and my face flushes. "Yes," I say honestly. "Thanks."

He drops my hair, and instantly, I wish his hands were back on me. What is *wrong* with me? I must be really hormonal. Maybe I'm pent-up from not having sex for seventeen whole years. Hmm. Only one way to fix that.

"So," Beckett says, standing up. "If that's it, I guess I'll be going."

"You're definitely not coming on the trip?"

"Nah," he says. "I never liked Florida. Too commercial."

What's that supposed to mean? "Yeah," I say. "Um. Well, thanks for the ride."

"You're welcome." He takes the helmet out of my hand and holds it by the chin strap. "Catch you later, Pink."

Then he turns and heads back to his motorcycle, throws his leg over the side, and drives away. I take another deep breath and then head inside. It's only then that I realize I left my carry-on in the compartment of Beckett's bike.

* * *

"There you are!" Derrick says once he spots me wandering around the gate where our flight is supposed to take off from. The whole area is a mess of my classmates. There doesn't seem to be any order or anyone in charge, which is actually good for me. Easier to sneak on the flight.

Derrick comes rushing over, his face filled with concern. He's wearing a dark-green sweater and baggy jeans and his face looks freshly shaven, and now that I'm here with him I feel relieved, like everything's going to be okay.

"I was so worried." He frowns and smooths my hair. "What's wrong, hon? You look pale."

"Do I?" I don't feel pale. In fact, I feel kind of . . . hot. It's definitely not from being close to Beckett, though. It's probably because I left my bag on his bike. And so now all I have is my purse. Good news = I have my cash, my debit card, and my ID. Bad news = my carry-on had some of my clothes, some underwear, my makeup, and my inappropriate bathing suit.

"Yeah." Derrick steps back and looks at me. "Your face is pale but your cheeks are red." He's holding a paper container of soft pretzel bites. Humph. I guess he wasn't so worried about me that he couldn't think about food.

"Why didn't you text me?" I demand as he follows me over to the self check-in. I swipe my debit card and grab my boarding pass. Ha! Try to keep me off the flight now, chaperones!

"My phone died." He holds up the blank screen. "I was

going to charge it when I got here, but then I realized I packed my charger in my suitcase."

"Oh." I take a deep breath and try to collect my thoughts. "Well, I missed the bus."

"You know you're not supposed to be getting on the flight then, right?" Derrick asks. "It was in the informational packet."

"Yeah, I know." I shrug, like it's no big deal. I'm starting to feel a lot better now that I'm inside and my stomach has stopped churning. And Beckett's probably right. Are they really going to stop me from getting on the plane? I doubt it. I reach out and grab one of Derrick's pretzel bites and dip it in the little cup of melted cheese sitting next to them. Yum.

"Was your mom pissed?"

"Pissed?"

"Yeah, that she had to drive you to the airport?"

"Oh. Um, no." I don't know why, but I don't want Derrick to know that Beckett drove me here. Not that Derrick would care. Derrick is not the type of guy who gets jealous. And he doesn't need to be. I love Derrick. I am going to marry Derrick. I am about to lose my virginity to Derrick. I should tell him. About Beckett. Now. He should know now. Tell him. Right now.

"I think we should have sex," I blurt. The girls who are sitting in the airport chairs a few feet away—Renee Hayes and Suri Cusimano—turn to look.

"*What?*" Derrick asks. He swallows the last pretzel bite and then throws the empty container in the trash.

I lean in close to him. "I mean, aren't you . . . I mean, don't you want to have sex with me?" I don't know why, but it's never occurred to me that maybe Derrick doesn't want to have sex with me. I always thought he was just being nice, waiting for me to decide that *I* wanted to.

"Of course I want to have sex with you," he says. "I just . . . I didn't think that was something you were, you know, interested in."

"You didn't think I was interested in sex?" What's that supposed to mean? Does he think I'm some kind of prude? Or asexual? Why would he think that? I always try to be really into it when we're making out. I read an article somewhere that said guys love enthusiasm. They just want to know you're enjoying what's going on. You don't even have to be that good at what you're doing as long as you're enthusiastic.

Of course, I read that article in the eighth grade, before I'd even kissed a boy. Quinn, Aven, and I stole Quinn's mom's *Cosmo* and we were reading all the articles about sex, especially the ones where guys would list the top one hundred things they wanted women to do to them. (That was definitely a little scary to read when you're in eighth grade. You really do not want to think about some of the things that guys want you to do when you're that young. Actually, I don't want to think about some of them now. La, la, la, not thinking about it.)

"I don't know." Derrick seems all excited now. His eyes are sparkling, and he licks his lips. "You just never brought it up before."

"Well, *you* never brought it up before."

He leans in even closer to me. "So does this mean, you know, that you're ready?" He's practically salivating.

"I don't know," I say, even though obviously I've already decided that I am. But I have to keep at least a little bit of the mystery alive, don't I? I don't know why, but something about Beckett driving me here has made me even more convinced that I'm ready to sleep with Derrick. It doesn't make any sense. Why would coming here with Beckett make me realize I want to have sex with Derrick? Also, I have to admit that I like the way Derrick's looking at me right now. Almost like he doesn't know me. Like he's shocked at what I'm capable of. I raise my eyebrow and bite my lip in what I hope is a sexy way.

"Okay, well, I know a way to—" Derrick starts.

"Lyla!" someone screams. It's a voice that's familiar but not at the same time, almost like hearing something in a dream. "Lyla! There you are!"

I look up to see Aven Shepard calling my name from the other side of the room. I frown. Why is she calling my name? Yes, we used to be best friends, but honestly, I can't remember the last time I talked to Aven. Actually, that's not true. If I'm being completely honest, I do remember the last time I talked to Aven. We were coming down the stairs after eighth period last year, and she bumped into me, and then I said, "Excuse you!" and then she said, "Excuse me," in this really small voice, and I remember I was so annoyed at her for not sounding annoyed, because Aven is always trying to be, like, the victim.

She's always acting like she never does anything wrong when, if you ask me, she does a lot of things wrong. She just doesn't want to admit it to herself. Anyway. That was back when our friendship was so fresh in my mind that any inter-action I had with her automatically got logged in my brain, like I was just buying time until we were going to be friends again. But of course we never are.

"Oh," I say. "Ummm . . . hi."

"Listen," she says. Her light-brown hair is pulled to one side in a fishtail braid, and she's wearing khaki shorts and a navy-blue T-shirt. Isn't she cold? I know we're going to Flor-ida, but why is she wearing her Florida outfit now? "I need to talk to you." She holds her phone up and bites her bottom lip. "Did you get your email?"

"Sorry," Derrick says, looking at her. He shakes his head. "Aven, right? Sorry, Aven, but we're talking here. And it's kind of private." Wow. He sounds very serious. I've never heard him sound so serious before. I flush with pleasure. He must really want to have sex with me if he's sounding so serious.

Aven swallows. "Oh," she says. "I'm sorry, I didn't . . . I mean, I didn't realize you were talking." But she doesn't move. She just takes in another deep breath and stands there. "It's just . . . did you get your email?"

"My email?"

"Yeah, the ones we sent? Did you get it?" Her voice sounds frazzled, and she shifts her weight from foot to foot, like she's here asking about a secret government document and not just some dumb email we sent when we were fourteen. Her hair is a lot longer than it used to be, and it's darker on the top than the bottom. She must have gotten an ombre. It makes her look older. In a good way.

"What email?" Derrick asks.

Oh, god.

"Yes," I say to Aven. "I got it." I say it firmly, like the conversation is over and that's all I have to say on the matter. This isn't going to turn into one of those trips down memory lane, where we reminisce about how crazy everything was when we were fourteen, and oh my god can you believe we sent those things, and holy crap weren't we so young, and maybe we should just be friends again or at least if we're not friends, we should just forget about everything and no hard feelings when we go to college okay mm-hmm bye.

I thrust my chin in the air and force myself to meet her eyes, determined not to show her any emotion.

But my throat tightens and my heart starts beating fast. I remember her, standing in front of the school on the day we stopped being friends. *I'm not the one who told your mom, Lyla! I don't understand how you could be mad at me! It's not even anyone's fault.*

But of course it *was* her fault. Her and Quinn's fault, both. And no matter how much I miss both of them, no matter how much I think about them, it can never be the same. And so what's the point?

"Flight 935 to Sarasota is now boarding, Flight 935 to Sarasota is now boarding at Gate 24," a voice chirps over the loudspeaker.

"Well!" I say just as chirpily. "Here we go! I guess we better board."

"Where's your stuff?" Derrick asks, frowning. "Didn't you bring a carry-on?"

"Nope," I say. "Just this." I hold up my Coach wristlet, a present from Derrick for my seventeenth birthday last summer.

"That's all you brought for a carry-on?" Aven asks skeptically.

"I'm trying to simplify my life," I reply haughtily. "Everyone is so obsessed with materialism and *things*. I'm, you know, streamlining." I pet my Coach wristlet like it's the only thing I need in life. Which is really ridiculous when you think about it, because if someone were trying to strip down their existence, they really wouldn't leave themselves with a Coach wristlet. They'd probably get some kind of wallet made from recycled hemp or something.

"You're trying to streamline your life?" Aven asks, sounding even more incredulous. Like she knows me or something.

"A person can change," I say ominously. I try to look mysterious, like there are all kinds of things she doesn't know about me, all kinds of ways I've changed in the two years since we've stopped being friends.

"When did you decide to simplify your life?" Derrick asks. "Because you never told me that." He looks suspicious. "Is this why you want to have sex?"

"You want to have sex?" Aven asks. Her forehead crinkles. "Wait. You two haven't slept together yet? Haven't you been going out for forever?"

"Oh my god," I say, holding my hand up. "Both of you need to stop."

"Whatever," Aven says. She shakes her head. "Your sex life is none of my business."

"You're damn right it's not."

I turn and start to walk away, hoping they get the message. The message being that Derrick should follow me and Aven should just go away. But it doesn't work.

"Lyla," she says. "Please, wait. Can we . . . I mean, can I talk to you for a second?"

I sigh, then tilt my head back and roll my head around, trying to get rid of some of the tension in my shoulders. "What is it?"

She glances at Derrick. "Um, I want . . . can we talk in private?"

I almost laugh out loud. Funny that she's so worried about privacy now. I want to tell her no, but I have a feeling she's not going to give up.

"I'll be right back," I say to Derrick.

I walk a few feet away and cross my arms over my chest. "What is it?" I ask her. "Make it quick, we're about to board."

She nods, then fiddles with her hair. "I just wanted to know if you're going to do what the email says."

"Excuse me?"

"Are you taking it seriously? You know, about learning to trust? Because I'm thinking . . . I'm thinking that I'm going to be really, um, trying to do what mine says." She shakes her head. "In fact, I've kind of been waiting for a chance to do it."

I remember her email. The one she sent to herself.

Before graduation, I will . . . *tell the truth*.

I know exactly what she meant, too. While my email was ambiguous, hers was very specific. It was about Liam, the guy she's had a crush on for forever. She was going to tell him she was in love with him.

For a second, my heart softens, and I want to tell her

that we were just kids, that we just wrote things down without really thinking about them, without really knowing the repercussions. That if she's going to tell Liam that she loves him, she really needs to think about what that's going to do to their friendship, if it's worth the fact that things might change or that she might lose him.

But then I remember what she did to me, what she almost cost me.

And I feel my heart harden.

"Yeah, Aven," I say, sarcastically. "I'm really going to work on learning to trust. Because remember what happened when I trusted you? It didn't work out so well, remember?"

She looks like she's been slapped. "Lyla," she says. "I never wanted—"

"Save it," I say. "I didn't want to hear it then, and I don't want to hear it now."

I turn away and walk back toward Derrick.

"Everything okay?" he asks.

"Yeah," I say, even though my stomach is rolling. "I'll feel better when we're in Florida."

And when Aven Shepard is out of my sight.

When we get on the plane, Derrick changes seats with me so that I can have the one closest to the window. He takes my hand and pulls me close. I lean my head against his shoulder and breathe in his scent. Beckett and Aven start to fade into the back of my mind, and for the first time all morning, my heart rate slows to normal and I start to feel like myself.

"I'm so glad we're going on this trip together," I murmur.

"Me too," he says. His voice sounds more enthusiastic than usual. If we're being completely honest, Derrick didn't even really want to go to Florida. He wanted to go on some dumb baseball trip, which didn't make sense because he's not even on the baseball team. Derrick plays lacrosse. But all his friends play baseball, and they were going to Myrtle Beach to play in some tournament, and Derrick wanted to go too, which was so stupid because what the hell was he going to do down there while all his friends were playing baseball?

"What room number are you?" he asks.

"I don't know."

He reaches into his duffel and pulls out a sheaf of papers. "We got these on the bus," he says. "Room 145. I'm rooming with Beckett Cross and Liam Marsh."

Beckett. At the sound of his name, my stomach does a somersault. "You're rooming with Beckett?"

"Yeah. He's a cool guy. Liam too. They're definitely the types that would let us have the room to ourselves for a little bit."

"Beckett's not going on the trip," I say automatically. Don't ask me how I know, don't ask me how I know, don't ask me how I know.

"He's not?"

"No."

"Perfect." Derrick grins and doesn't ask me to elaborate. I guess the possibility of sex is making him a man of few words. "Then we'll definitely have a chance to have the room to ourselves. Who are you rooming with?"

"I don't know. Where did you get that paper?" I ask.

"I told you, they handed them out when we got on the bus," he says.

Shit. What with this whole maybe-having-sex-with-Derrick thing and then Aven coming up to me like that, I almost forgot that I'm not even supposed to be here. Although I'm already on the plane, so I really doubt they're going to make me get off. It was surprisingly easy to board. I just handed over my ticket like everyone else. None of our class chaperones even asked me why I wasn't on the bus. Talk about not keeping track of us. I mean, isn't that pretty irresponsible of the school?

I always see those links on Facebook to news stories about kids getting left behind in dangerous places by their schools, and I always wondered how the hell that could happen. Now I know. They don't pay any attention. To anything. But still. Just because they were so hands-off about boarding doesn't mean I want to call attention to myself.

"Do you think if I ask for my room assignment they're going to make me get off the plane?" I ask.

"Why would they make you get off the plane?" Derrick sounds panicked. Hmm. I wonder why he didn't seem as panicked when he thought I'd missed the bus. He was just calmly eating pretzel nuggets. He's probably nervous now because he knows he's going to get some sex.

"Because I wasn't on the bus!" I say, slightly exasperated. I know he has sex brain, but really. Try to keep up.

A head pops over the back of the seat in front of us. "*Hola!*" a voice says. It's my friend Juliana. Well, our friend Juliana. She was actually Derrick's friend first. Well, sort of. She was dating Derrick's friend Jasper and then they broke up, but somehow she stayed friends with Derrick. And now she's friends with me. Again, sort of. She's not the type of friend you can call up and, like, depend on for anything. First, she never answers her phone. And second, she has no boundaries. Like, for example, if I had called her this morning, she most likely wouldn't have answered her phone. And if I had, she would have refused to let me talk to Derrick until she found out all our business. She's nice. But she's kind of nosy.

"Are we excited to get crazy?" Juliana asks. Sometimes she talks in first-person plural.

"I am," I say. "I'm definitely ready to get crazy."

Juliana laughs and tosses her head back. Her long, dark curls hit the window.

I frown. "What's so funny?" Of course I'm ready to get crazy.

"Oh, nothing," she says. "Just, you know, thinking about you two getting crazy."

She looks at Derrick and gives him a secret little smile.

I glance over at him, and he shifts on his seat a little, looking uncomfortable. Could Juliana be talking about our sex life? Derrick wouldn't have told her we hadn't had sex, would he? That's, like, personal private information.

"Anyway," Juliana says, "I have a hookup for tonight. Party in my room." She winks at us and then drops back down into her seat.

I want to ask Derrick what she was talking about, but I decide to let it go. So what if he told Juliana we haven't had sex? It's not like she's a stranger. She's my friend, too. And besides, I'm not embarrassed about it. There's no reason to be embarrassed about not having sex yet. After this weekend, it won't be an issue anyway.

The pilot is on the speaker now, talking about how we should turn off all our electronic devices. So far not one teacher has even bothered me about being on this flight. They must have checked me off on some list when I boarded, but really? I wasn't on the bus. Doesn't anyone even want to ask me about it? This trip is definitely not well managed at all.

"So," Derrick says. He leans in close to me again. "What were we talking about?"

"Having sex," I say. The words feel foreign and delicious on my tongue. I mean, yes, I've talked about sex before, but not about me actually having it. Like, imminently. A dangerous little thrill runs up my spine.

"So you really want to?"

"Yes," I breathe. "I really want to."

And that's when Beckett Cross taps Derrick on the shoulder. "Excuse me," he says. He holds up my carry-on bag. "But Lyla left this on my motorcycle."

THREE

THE PROBLEM WITH LIES IS THAT THEY CAN end up making something totally innocent seem like more than it is. If I'd just told Derrick from the beginning that Beckett had driven me to the airport, it would have seemed like I had nothing to hide. Which I didn't. Which I don't.

And then Derrick wouldn't have had to find out when Beckett showed up on the plane holding my bag. Of course, it also didn't help that Beckett said that I'd left my bag on the back of his motorcycle. It was very inflammatory language when you think about it. Saying you left something on someone's motorcycle sounds very covert and sexy, like maybe you left it there after a night of passion.

Of course, not only had I lied about how I got to the airport, I'd also lied and said I was minimizing my life instead of just admitting I'd forgotten my carry-on. (That was a really ridiculous lie. I'm shocked I was so brazen about it. If

Derrick hadn't been so tantalized by the prospect of having sex with me, he wouldn't have believed it for a second. I'm, like, the most materialistic person around, and everyone knows it. Even Aven couldn't believe it, and she always tries to see the best in people.)

"I wasn't riding around with him," I say. "Beckett was just at the school when I got there late, and so he drove me."

"He *drove* you?" Derrick asks.

"Yes. I mean, no. I mean, yes." I don't know why, but suddenly I'm confused. He's making it sound like Beckett driving me was doing something bad. It's like a double entendre or something, even though it's not.

"Well, which is it?" Derrick demands.

We're having this fight as we walk into the Sand Dollar Siesta Hotel. It's a very inopportune time to be having a fight, because all I really want to do is enjoy the fact that I'm in Florida. As soon as we stepped out of the airport, the warm air soothed my soul and the humidity tickled my nose and made my skin feel like it was getting a much-needed drink.

The whole flight here Derrick just sat there in stony silence while I tried not to think about the fact that Beckett had come all the way back to the airport just to bring me my bag. Of course I knew Beckett hadn't come back *just* for me. He must have come back because he'd decided to go on the trip after all. He wouldn't have come back just to give me my stuff.

Although if I'm being completely honest, thinking about Beckett coming back just for me gave me a tiny bit of a thrill. It didn't help that he'd been sitting a few aisles over from us on the plane, and that he'd sent me a drink from the stewardess—a cranberry with Sprite (pink!) accompanied by a note that said, *Pink—Sorry if I got you in trouble. Tell your boyfriend to chill out from me. ~B*

Of course I had to show Derrick the note, because if I hadn't, he would have gotten all suspicious. But then when he read it, he got even more mad and demanded to know why the note was addressed to Pink, and then I said it was because Beckett didn't know my name. Which I thought would actually make Derrick feel better, because really, how could anything scandalous be going on if Beckett didn't even know my name? But this just incensed Derrick even more. He said it was more insulting that I was lying to him about a guy who didn't know my name, and that *of course* Beckett knew my name, and that he must have just been pretending he didn't to play a mind game with me.

Which didn't make any sense, because why would Beckett want to play a mind game with me? So then I told Derrick he was being a little bit crazy, so then *Derrick* said it was completely inappropriate for another guy to give me a nickname, and then he just sat there and refused to talk to me for the rest of the flight, and then kept it up for the whole bus ride from the airport to the hotel.

He even made me carry my own suitcase, which was super annoying. Hasn't he ever heard of chivalry? You'd think after I'd pretty much just agreed to have sex with him, he'd at least carry my suitcase.

"Hello?" Derrick says now. "Are you going to answer me?"

"I forgot the question," I say honestly. I'm distracted now because as we're walking, one of my shoes is acting funny. I look down to see that the part of my flip-flop that goes between my toes has started to come loose. Great. That's what I get for changing my shoes as soon as we got on the bus to the hotel. How do people who are simplifying their lives deal with their shoes breaking down? Probably they don't even wear shoes. Or the ones they do are made from extra-strong raw materials.

"The question *is*, why didn't you tell me that you drove over here with him? It makes it seem like you wanted to hide it."

"I didn't want to hide it," I say. I'm limping now. "Can we sit down for a minute?" I ask irritably. "My shoe is falling apart."

I hobble over to one of the benches in front of the hotel and rummage through my carry-on bag, looking for my spare shoes. I pull them out, a pair of simple pink flip-flops.

Derrick sits down on the bench next to me. "Look," he says. "I don't . . . I'm not mad. I mean, I am mad, but . . .

maybe we should take some time to think about this."

"To think about what?" I wiggle my toes in the new shoes. Much better.

"You know, the whole . . . sex thing."

"You want to think about the whole sex thing?"

"Yeah. I mean, we need to ask ourselves if we really should be having sex when you just lied to me."

"I didn't lie to you!"

"You lied by omission. Which is just as bad." He sighs and stands up. "I just don't think we should rush into anything."

"We're not rushing into it," I say. "We've been going out for two years! In fact, when you think about it, it's completely ridiculous that we haven't done it yet. We're, like, stunted."

"*I'm* not stunted," he says, sounding offended.

It takes me a second to realize what he's saying. That he's not stunted but I am. Just because he's not a virgin. Just because he had sex with Lucia Santos at the beginning of sophomore year. Just before we got together.

"I don't mean each of us," I say defensively. "I mean our relationship."

This makes him mad. "You think our relationship is stunted?"

"No, that's not what—"

"Are you two coming?" Mr. Beals, my AP bio teacher and one of our chaperones, asks us. He's standing just inside the automatic doors at the front of the hotel, looking for stragglers. "We're meeting in the conference room for an informational meeting." His eyes widen when he sees me. "Lyla McAfee," he says. "Were you on the bus?"

"Yes," I say. "But I never got my room assignment. I think maybe I was overlooked somehow."

He frowns, and his eyebrows knit together. His teacher sense is telling him something's off about the situation, but he can't really come right out and accuse me of lying, because he has no proof.

"Mr. Beals!" Janae Patt squeals, running up to him. "You need to come quick. Bruno James might have ringworm, and it's, like, so contagious! We probably all have it. I think he needs to get to a doctor ASAP."

Mr. Beals sighs. "Okay, guys," he says to me and Derrick. "Please come inside. Lyla, we'll get you your room assignment. Just please, come inside."

I think about making a joke about how I don't want to come inside if Bruno James has ringworm, but something about the look on Mr. Beals's face makes me stop. The poor guy isn't even going to be able to enjoy his time in Florida because he's going to be dealing with our crazy senior class.

I stand up. "You coming?" I ask Derrick. I step closer to him, putting my arms around his waist and making sure to push my chest against his. Wow. When did I become such a sexual vixen? "We can talk about this a little later. After the meeting, we can go to our rooms and change into our suits. Then we can hit the beach."

"No," Derrick says. He takes my arms and removes them from around his waist.

"No?"

"No." He shakes his head. "I'm sorry, Lyla, but I need a little time to think about this. I'll text you later, okay?" He kisses my forehead (my forehead! WTF?) and then pushes by me and into the hotel.

The informational meeting is a complete joke, filled with rules no one's going to follow, and it's cut short because of the Bruno James ringworm scandal. It turns out I'm assigned to room 217, which is nice, because all the second-floor rooms have balconies overlooking the beach. When I get to my room, my roommates aren't there yet, so I take a second to step out onto the balcony and take in the scene.

Miles of white sand stretch out in either direction, inter-rupted only by colorful beach umbrellas. The beach is busy, but not crazy—there are just enough people to make it look fun and happening, but not enough to make it too crowded, with no place to put your blanket. Not that I have a blanket. Hmmm.

I look down at the piece of paper in my hand, the one Mr. Beals handed me downstairs all absentminded-like while he was looking at Bruno James's leg. Which definitely looked like it had ringworm. It was all burrowed into his skin, and like, *round*. Like a worm. Mr. Beals definitely looked disturbed. When I left to head up to my room, they were calling the hotel doctor down to take a look.

Lyla McAfee, the paper says. *Room 217.* I wonder who my roommates are. Since I got my room assignment late, Mr. Beals just scribbled it down on a piece of paper for me.

The rooms are triples, with two double beds and a cot in each one. I wonder if it would be rude to put my stuff down on one of the beds before my roommates get here. I mean, shouldn't it be first come, first serve? On the other hand, the last thing I want to do is get them mad by staking my claim.

I take in a deep breath and sit down on one of the beds. I leave my carry-on sitting on the floor, so it seems like I've kind of taken ownership of the bed without actually taking ownership of it. The doors to the balcony are open, and a breeze flows through the room. There's a fancy bottle of water and a sweet-looking clementine on my pillow, along with a tiny silver sunshine charm. *Welcome to Florida,* it says in lime-green lettering, *the Sunshine State.*

Everything is so cheerful and bright here!

But I don't feel cheerful or bright.

All I can think about is Derrick.

What am I supposed to do until he calls me? And what about his phone? He said it was dead. How long will it take him to charge it? Twenty minutes? An hour? Will he plug it in right when he gets to his room? Will he text me while it's charging, or is he going to wait until it's fully charged? He'll probably wait until it's fully charged. Boys are so stupid like that. He probably doesn't even realize he can just text me while it's plugged in. He probably doesn't—

The door to the hotel room goes flying open and Quinn Reynolds appears in front of me. Oh, god. First Aven at the airport, and now Quinn. What is this, some kind of nightmare?

She looks me up and down, her cool blue eyes taking me in. I remember those eyes. I remember how in the seventh grade Michael Masters told Quinn her eyes were beautiful, and I was so jealous I could hardly stand it. I went home and begged and begged my mom to let me get colored contacts, but she refused. I don't even wear contacts—my vision is perfect—but I saw an advertisement online that said you could get them even if you didn't need vision correction.

It just seemed so unfair for Quinn to have those gorgeous eyes when she wasn't even interested in boys. All she was interested in was school. And getting into Stanford. And becoming . . . whatever it was that she wanted to become. First it was a doctor, then a lawyer, then an accountant, then a surgeon, then some kind of gene specialist. She could never just pick a normal job, like a teacher or something. No, Quinn had to be glamorous.

At least when it came to her careers.

"You've got to be kidding me," she says now. She drops her suitcase on the floor and then walks into the bathroom and shuts the door.

Well.

That is definitely not the Quinn I remember. The Quinn I remember was afraid of making anyone upset and always knew the right thing to say. She always did the right thing, even if it was hard or uncomfortable.

Except when she told your secret.

The sound of water running comes floating through the bathroom door, and then finally she emerges. She doesn't look at me and instead just walks across the room to her suitcase, which she lifts up and drops onto the other bed.

"I'm assuming you took that bed?" she asks as she rummages through her clothes.

"Um, well, I'm not sure. I mean, I didn't want to take it before everyone else got here, so I just thought that maybe—"

"Well, whatever," she says, cutting me off. "You can have it. Let Aven sleep on the cot."

"Aven?"

"Yeah." Quinn pulls out a blue one-piece bathing suit, a gauzy white cover-up, and a pair of beaded flip-flops. "She's our third roommate."

"You have got to be kidding me." Who's in charge of making these room assignments anyway? I'd like to meet whoever it is, because they must have a really screwed-up sense of humor. Not that any of the teachers know that Quinn, Aven, and I used to be best friends. Actually, maybe they do. And this is their sick way of getting back at us for having to come on this trip and not have any fun.

"Yup," Quinn says. She shakes her head sadly. "Apparently she's still living in fantasy world."

"What do you mean?"

"Aven was in charge of making the room assignments. She's on the Student Action Committee."

"The Student Action Committee?" Never heard of it. "I've never even heard of the Student Action Committee."

"That's not surprising," Quinn says, shaking her head again.

"What's that supposed to mean?"

"Nothing, just that sometimes you don't pay attention to what's going on."

"Yeah," I say. "And sometimes *you* pay *too* much attention to what's going on."

She opens her mouth to say something, but then she must realize what I'm really talking about. Our fight. The way she told my secret, how she almost cost me my relationship with my mom, how she might be the reason I haven't talked to my dad in over two years

"Whatever," Quinn says. She disappears into the bathroom again. When she emerges, she's wearing her bathing suit and cover-up, along with the beaded flip-flops and a floppy brown hat. The hat looks ridiculous. But Quinn has fair skin (to go along with those gorgeous blue eyes), and she burns really easily.

"I like your hat," I say, just to be a brat.

But Quinn either doesn't get the sarcasm or doesn't care. She starts taking her clothes out of her suitcase and refolding each piece carefully before placing them in the top dresser drawer.

"You're unpacking?" I ask.

"Yes, Lyla, I'm unpacking. It's what one does when they get to a place they're staying. Most people don't throw their things around like hooligans, even though I'm sure it's just so tempting."

I want to tell her it's ridiculous to unpack your things at a hotel, that nobody does that, especially if they're only staying for a few days, but I'm not sure if it's true. Am I the weird one? Does everyone unpack their things at a hotel?

There's a beep as someone slides their key card into our room door. The handle slides down and Aven walks in. She looks around the room. I glare at her, wanting to show my displeasure over the fact that she made us roommates. But if she has any embarrassment about it, she doesn't show it. In fact, she doesn't even try to hide her happiness. Her cheeks are all rosy and her hair is a little tangled and her eyes are bright. Her skin looks flushed, like maybe she ran up the stairs to get here.

She sees that Quinn and I have each snagged a bed, and I brace myself for a fight. Well, if she pitches a fit about it, there's no way I'm going to take the cot. Aven should take it, as punishment for putting us all in this mess. Not that it would be a big deal for me to take the cot—I'll probably be spending most of my time with Derrick in his room, anyway. (Well, once we make up from our fight.) Now that I know I'm rooming with Aven and Quinn, there's no way I'm going to be able to have this room to myself. I'm not asking them for any favors.

We'll just have to use Derrick's room. It shouldn't be a problem, even though Beckett's here now. In fact, Beckett owes me for getting me in trouble with Derrick, so he'll probably be happy to let me and Derrick have the room to ourselves for a few hours. A few hours? Is that how long it will take?

Not the actual sex part. I mean, I know that won't take a few hours. Will it? That seems rather unpleasant. But you'd think we'd have dinner or something first, like out on the balcony. Ooh, maybe by candlelight! Derrick will order up some lobster or something from downstairs (is there even a restaurant downstairs?—I make a mental note to check), and it will be fresh from the ocean and we'll sit on the balcony and eat and smell the salty air.

He'll have ordered chocolate cake (my favorite) for dessert, but by the time we're done eating our main course, there will be way too much anticipation, and I'll be all, "Let's just skip dessert, don't you think?" and then his eyes will get all bright the way they do when he's excited, and he'll take my hand and lead me into the bedroom and then—

"I guess I'm taking the cot," Aven says, not sounding put-upon at all. She drops her things on the cot, then stands in front of us and twists her hands together. "I just want you guys to know that I'm really happy we're all rooming together."

Quinn and I stare at her blankly.

"I think we could all benefit from spending some time together," Aven goes on. "I know that our misunderstanding got out of hand, but with graduation coming up, I think it might really be time to move past it."

I can't help but laugh. "That's what you think it was? A misunderstanding?" Yeah, if a misunderstanding is your two friends taking something you told them in confidence and then almost ruining your whole life when it turned out they couldn't keep their mouths shut.

"I know your feelings are still probably really hurt, Lyla," Aven says, her tone getting serious. "But Quinn and I never meant to hurt you."

"Don't speak for me," Quinn says.

I glare at her. "So you did mean to hurt me?"

"Whatever," Quinn says. "I don't want to do this. I don't even *care* about this. It takes up, like, this amount of space in my mind." She picks up her fingers and holds them about a centimeter apart, to show us just how little she thinks of it. And then, without saying anything else, she turns and walks out of the room. A second later, she peeks her head back in the door.

"Keep your hands off my stuff, Aven," she says. "I know you like to borrow people's things." She gives us this really big fake smile and then walks out.

Aven's lip quivers for a second, like maybe she's going to cry. "Lyla," she says. "Can we just—"

I hold my hand up. "No," I say. "Let's make this easy. I didn't want to forgive you then, and I still don't want to forgive you now. So save whatever dumb thing you're about to say."

Her eyes fill with tears, but she shakes them off. "Forget it," Aven says bitterly. "Just forget it. I was stupid to think that maybe you'd changed even a little bit."

"*Me?*" I say. "I'm the one who has to change?"

"You don't get it, Lyla. You really don't. In fact, you're just as selfish as you used to be." Then she turns and walks out the door, slamming it behind her.

I sit there for a second, stunned. How did this happen? This morning everything seemed so . . . I don't know, *possible*. I was going on a senior trip to sunny Florida to lose my virginity to my boyfriend who loved me. Now I'm in a big fight with said boyfriend and stuck in a hotel room by myself. A room I have to share with my two ex-best friends. It's ridiculous.

I pick up my phone and think about calling Juliana. But I'm really not in the mood to hang out with her, especially not after the comment she made on the plane. But if I don't hang out with Juliana, then who am I supposed to hang out with? After Aven and Quinn and I stopped being friends, it was hard to make new ones. It wasn't like I could just insert myself into someone else's group. They'd all built memories and stories and private jokes and connections. I started dating Derrick pretty soon after my fight with Aven and Quinn, and then I was spending so much time with him I guess I never really had to worry about replacing them.

I pick up my phone just to double-check that Derrick hasn't texted or called. No texts. No missed calls. Should I text him? Or call him? Or maybe I should just go and see him. What was his room number again? I think he said 145.

Of course, that would be presumptuous, since he basically told me to leave him alone. Unless I wore my inappropriate bathing suit. That might cause him to decide he was done thinking about things with us, that he'd had enough time to ruminate over my lies. I pull my bathing suit out of my bag and lay it out on the bed.

Beckett will be there, a little voice in my head whispers.

So what? I don't care if Beckett sees me in my bikini. I mean, I was planning on wearing it in front of all those strangers on the beach. Beckett's probably not even in his room, anyway. Derrick probably punched him as soon as he got there. He was probably like, "You need to stay away from my girlfriend, Beckett!" and even though Beckett has no interest in me, like, whatsoever, that won't stop Derrick from knocking him out.

The thought of two guys fighting over me is kind of exciting. I know violence is never really the answer, but—

There's a knock on the door, and I spring off the bed.

Derrick!

I smooth my hair down and then arrange it over my shoulders so that it falls perfectly around my face.

I throw the door open.

But it's not Derrick.

It's Beckett.

"Hey, Pink," he says, and leans against the door frame. "What's good?"

FOUR

I WILL NOT LOOK AT HIS BICEPS, I WILL NOT look at his biceps, I will not look at his biceps. I keep repeating this to myself, like a mantra. Because the way Beckett is standing, with his arm against the door frame, is making his biceps look all kinds of muscular and delicious.

Okay. Deep breaths. I need to get him out of here as soon as possible. Yes, he did me a favor by bringing me to the airport this morning, but he also really screwed things up by sending me that note. Who does something like that?

"What do you want?" I ask, making sure to keep my voice clipped.

He shrugs. "To make sure you got your stuff okay." He pushes by me and into the room. "Nice room," he says, looking around.

"I'm sure it's the same as yours." I don't shut the door, because I don't want him to get the idea that he can just stay here, like, *lingering.* He needs to leave. What if Derrick comes by? That would be disastrous. I poke my head into the hallway and make sure no one saw him come in. Phew. Coast clear.

"No, it's different." Beckett crosses the room and walks right out onto the balcony. "Nice view," I hear him say.

If he thinks I'm going to follow him out there, he's mistaken. He's like a dog—if you reward him when he's acting up, he'll think he can get away with it. A few seconds go by, then half a minute, then a minute, then two. What is he *doing* out there?

"Well," I say real loud. "Thanks for checking on me, but I'm kind of on my way out."

"What?" he calls. "I can't hear you from out here."

I take a deep breath in through my nose and out through my mouth. It's a trick I learned in a yoga class I took last year. It was a phys ed elective, which was kind of a joke. It's impossible to feel relaxed and Zen when you're sitting in the disgusting-smelling gym with boys playing basketball on the other side of the divider.

"I said I'm on my way out," I call. "So I'll have to see you later." It's a lie, of course. I don't plan on seeing him later. Why would I want to see him later? Do I want to see him later? God, this trip is really not off to a good start.

"But you're seeing me now," he calls back. He sounds legitimately confused.

Well. Whatever. I'm not going out there. He can just sit there on the balcony as far as I'm concerned. Forever and ever. I'm not going to be following him around like some kind of sick puppy. I'm sure that's what he's used to, from all the stupid girls he's dated. He's probably convinced I'm going to come running out after him. Ha! Well, he definitely has another thing coming.

"So I noticed you have an inappropriate bathing suit laid out on your bed," he calls. "Are you planning on wearing that anytime soon?"

I run out onto the balcony.

"What?"

He's leaning over the side, inhaling the fresh air. A palm tree rustles in the breeze, sending the smell of sand and beach and ocean through the humid air. I cannot believe I am in this beautiful place and this is what I'm dealing with.

"Look," he says, turning around. "I'm not judging you or anything. I just think that if you're using that bathing suit to get attention from guys, you're going to attract the wrong kind of guys."

"I don't need to attract attention from guys," I say. "I have a boyfriend."

"And you have to use a skimpy bathing suit to get his attention?"

"No!"

He frowns. "Then you *do* want to get attention from other guys?"

"No!" I take a second to gather my thoughts. "I'm wearing the bathing suit for me."

"For you?"

"Yeah, you know, to feel good about myself." It's a canned answer, obviously. There's no way I would wear a bathing suit like that just to feel good about myself. No one feels good about themselves in a bathing suit like that, unless you're a bikini model. You're too worried about sucking in your stomach and how your thighs look.

"You have to wear a bathing suit like that to feel good about yourself?"

"Look," I say, annoyed now. "My swimwear is really none of your business."

He nods seriously. "Fair enough."

"Now, if you'll excuse me, I have to be somewhere."

"Where?"

"I was just about to call my friend Juliana," I say. "She's having a party tonight, and I have to get the details from her."

"Forget the party," Beckett says, shaking his head. "Come hang out with me instead."

"You have got to be kidding me," I say. "I'm not going anywhere with you."

"Why not?" He seems confused.

"Because." I cross my arms over my chest and look at him. "You're creepy."

"I'm *creepy*?"

"Yes." I tick off the reasons on my fingers. "One, you drive a motorcycle. Two, you showed up at my room unannounced. And three, you have a preoccupation with my swimwear." I take in another yoga breath. "Not to mention that talking to you is like talking to a three-year-old."

"Yeah, well, talking to you is like talking to a forty-year-old. You need to loosen up." But he doesn't sound mad. Or exasperated. Or anything. He just sounds kind of . . . amused. And he's looking at me with this little smirk on his face, like he has a secret about me.

I think about how he saw my inappropriate bathing suit. Then I think about how he asked me if I was going to be wearing it soon. Goose bumps break out on my arms, and I take in another long, slow, deep breath. "I think you should go." But my voice doesn't sound like I mean it.

"I think you should come with me," he says, with that same maddening grin on his face. Then he shakes his head. "Actually, no. I *know* you're going to come with me."

"Oh, yeah? And why is that?" God, he is so cocky.

"Because," he says, and shrugs his beautifully sculpted shoulders. "I know where Derrick is."

"Derrick's in his room."

"No, he isn't. He left with Lincoln Shrute."

"Where did they go?" A slightly panicked feeling begins rising in my chest.

"Come with me," Beckett says, "and I'll show you."

"You're lying. Derrick wouldn't have left without me." He wouldn't have. Derrick doesn't do things like that. He doesn't just . . . leave. Not without calling or texting to let me know. He just . . . he's not a normal boyfriend. He's *nice*.

He said he wanted space.

Beckett shrugs. "You don't have to believe me. But if I leave, and you're wrong, you might miss the rest of the day with him. Are you really going to take that chance?"

I take in a deep breath.

Before graduation, I will . . . learn to trust.

That stupid email. Why the hell am I thinking about it now? I *don't* trust Beckett. And besides, that email definitely wasn't talking about learning to trust shady guys who I've never had any history with. Was it? I'm beginning to get really confused. I think the humidity might be starting to get to me.

"Fine," I say, grabbing my purse from the nightstand. "I'm coming with you. But you're taking me right to Derrick. No funny business."

Beckett looks at me like I'm an insane person. "I don't believe in funny business," he says.

It's a lie, of course.

But what can I do?

I shake my head and follow him out of my room.

Before we get to the elevator, I send Derrick a text.

Where r u?

Trust or not, you have to make sure you cover all your bases.

Outside the hotel, the cobblestone walk is done in shades of orange and pink, giving it kind of a tropical feel. It's so pretty, and not something you'd ever see back in the Northeast, where gray and beige seem to be the colors of choice when it comes to architecture.

As soon as my feet hit the first step, my phone's ringing. My mom.

I'm tempted to send it to voice mail, but if I don't answer it, my mom might freak out. She's the type who does that kind of thing—can't get in touch with me for one minute and then does something totally off the rails, like calls the school to find out exactly where I am. You'd think it would mean she's overly involved in my life, but it's actually the opposite—my mom is out to lunch half the time, so when she can't get in touch with me, it snaps her back to reality and she immediately thinks she's lost me somewhere.

"Who's that?" Beckett asks, all nosy.

"No one." My hand hovers over the button. Should I answer or not answer? I don't want Beckett to hear me on the phone with my mom. First, because I'm going to have to lie, and second, because it's just . . . I don't know, weird to have a guy hear you talking on the phone to your parents.

I sigh and answer. "Oh, hi, Mom!" I say happily. I quickly run down in my head the list of things she might ask about, and then try to answer all her questions before she can ask them. "The flight was great, I got here no problem, everything's good!" My voice sounds slightly frantic.

"Oh, good," she says. "I'm so glad. So the late-bus thing worked out then?"

"Mm-hmm."

"Hi, Lyla's mom!" Beckett yells.

"Who's that?" my mom asks.

I ignore her. "So, ah, our class is about to take a trip down to the ocean. You know, to study some wildlife. The marine kind."

"Oh, that sounds nice," she says.

"It is."

"Come on, Lyla!" Beckett yells. "We better get going, the marine wildlife isn't going to wait. It has places to be."

"Who is that?" my mom asks again. "Is that Derrick?"

"Um, no, that's . . . that's just my lab partner. For our marine wildlife project. Anyway, I should get going. Call me later, okay?" I trust that she won't call me later, since she'll be back to focusing on herself probably as soon as we hang up.

"Marine wildlife?" Beckett asks, amused.

"Yeah," I say, daring him to ask me more. "I had to say something to get her off the phone."

"Hey, I'm not judging." He holds his hands up, like he couldn't care less what I tell my mom, even though he so was judging. "Even if you are shady."

I gape at him. "I'm not shady!"

"You kind of are."

"How am I shady?"

"You lied to your mom about there being a late bus. You got onto my motorcycle when you don't even know me. And you just told your mom about some bullshit marine wildlife project." He ticks the reasons off on his fingers. "Oh! And you packed an inappropriate bathing suit."

"Those things don't make me shady," I say. "They make me cool."

He grins. "Touché."

But before I can reply, I see something down the street that makes me stop.

Juliana. She's holding a plastic grocery bag and talking loudly into her cell phone. I freeze. Oh, god. The last thing I need is for Juliana to see me with Beckett. She's definitely not going to keep it a secret from Derrick. She has a big mouth.

I watch as she stops on the sidewalk and sort of shades her eyes from the glare of the sun. I can't tell if she sees me, or if she's looking at something else.

"Shit," I swear. I grab Beckett's arm and pull him into a souvenir shop.

"What the hell are you doing?" he yells as I drag him to the back of the store.

"Shh!" I hiss. "She might see us."

"Who might see us?"

"Just . . . this girl."

I crouch down behind a rack of sundresses and give him an expectant look.

"You have got to be kidding me."

I yank at his arm until he finally sighs and crouches down next to me. "Why are we doing this again?" he asks.

"My friend Juliana," I say. "She was out there on the street. And if she sees me with you, there's going to be trouble."

"What kind of trouble?" he asks. He looks doubtful, like the kind of thing I'd think is trouble is really going to be nothing.

"She's friends with Derrick."

"So?"

"*So* she'll tell him we were hanging out."

He shakes his head. "It's really sad that you and Derrick have such a non-trusting relationship."

"Well, when you sent me that note on the plane, it kind of made it sound like something was going on between us."

He rolls his eyes, like the idea is preposterous, and I try not to feel offended. "Look, is this really necessary?" he asks.

"I mean, look at yourself. You're hiding in the back of a store behind some nightgowns."

"They aren't nightgowns," I correct. "They're sundresses." I reach out and finger one. The material is soft and slides through my fingers. They're so pretty. I wonder if Beckett would mind if we stopped to buy one on the way out. "And if you knew Juliana, you would understand."

"What do you mean?"

"She's always in his business."

"Oh," he says knowingly. "She's in love with him."

"No, she's not in love with him," I say, shaking my head at how wrong he has it.

"A girl who's so worried about what you're doing? Who's friends with Derrick? She's definitely in love with him."

I ignore him and pop my head up over the sundresses and glance around the store: a family with a few kids, a middle-aged couple sifting through a bin of seashells, and a shirtless man with a huge belly looking at the beach chairs.

"There's no one here," I say, relieved. "She probably just—"

Juliana steps into my line of sight. She's off the phone now and looking around the store suspiciously, her eyes flitting over the rows of beachwear.

Beckett pops his head up next to me and starts looking around.

"Get down!" I screech. "Get down right now!"

For once, he listens. I watch as Juliana starts wandering

up and down the aisles, looking around. Crap. She obviously saw me come in here. She keeps walking, getting closer and closer to where we are. No way can I have her catch me crouched down here with Beckett. It makes me look way too guilty. I stand up quickly and pretend to be looking through the sundresses.

"Jesus," Beckett hisses. "What the hell are you doing? She's definitely going to see you now."

"Yes, but at least she won't catch me with *you*." I move away from the rack of dresses, forcing myself to walk slow and casual, even though my heart feels like it's going to beat right out of my chest. I head toward a display of little figurines made of sand and pick one up, studying it intently, like I'm really interested in buying it. Wow. Fourteen ninety-nine. For this little thing? That's ridiculous. It's probably not even made out of real sand. It's probably made out of some synthetic substitute, the kind that can kill your child or your dog if they accidentally put it in their mouth. I turn it over, and sure enough, *MADE IN CHINA* is stamped in capital letters on the bottom.

They should be ashamed of themselves.

I keep it in my hand, though, because suddenly, I can feel Juliana's eyes on me. She's watching as I turn the sand castle over and over in my hand. It's a little disconcerting, actually, the way I can feel her eyes boring into me. She has a very penetrating stare.

I wonder if Beckett's right, if she's really in love with Derrick. Has she been in love with him this whole time? Is she about to go crazy with passion and have some kind of psychotic break? I have a vision of her stomping over here and ripping the sand castle out of my hand and then using it to bash my head in. They'll have to call the police. And my mom. And my mom will have to come down here, and it will probably take her forever because she'll have to talk it over with her therapist and find out if it's a good idea. At least, I think she would. That's the problem with her self-realizations. She always has to—

"Yo," a voice breathes into my ear.

I jump. I was so distracted that I didn't realize Juliana is right next to me. Way to stay aware, Lyla. Everyone knows the first rule of avoiding getting caught doing something bad is to be alert. "Oh," I say dumbly. I instinctively take a step back, and my hand squeezes around the sand castle I'm holding.

"Hey," she says, giving me a huge grin. "What's up, girl?"

"Oh, not much," I say, "just looking for souvenirs. To, like, bring back to my mom."

"Oh, good idea." She reaches out and takes the sand castle out of my hand. "This is cute. But there's a used bookstore down the street. Maybe they'll have some obscure psychology book or something."

Annoyance sparks inside me as I realize Derrick must

have told her about my mom's path to self-discovery. "Thanks," I say.

Juliana pushes her long curls away from her face. "So I thought I saw you come in here with Beckett Cross."

"Umm . . ." I think about it, wondering if I should just tell her the truth. I mean, there's nothing wrong with what I'm doing. In fact, Beckett is taking me to Derrick. It's the only way I have to find him, actually. But I can't take the chance that Juliana is going to get to Derrick first and spin the story. "No," I say. I pretend to be peering around the store. "I mean, I think I saw him come in here. But he wasn't with me."

She bites her lip. Her teeth are blindingly white and perfectly shaped. "Okay," she says slowly. She leans in close to me, like she's going to tell me a secret. My first instinct is to back away, but something tells me that if I do that, it's going to infuriate her. So I force myself to stay where I am.

"You know," she says, "Beckett is not a nice guy."

"Well, I don't even know Beckett," I say wildly. "I mean, of course I *know* him. He's in some of my AP classes. But I don't, like, *know him* know him. I've only maybe spoken, like, five words to him." Shut up, Lyla! Shut up!

"That's good," Juliana says. "Because Derrick is such a nice guy, and you guys are awesome together." She puts her hand on my arm, like she's worried about me. "I just hope you guys can work this out. I know he really cares about you."

No, I want to yell. He doesn't just care about me. He loves me! We're about to have sex! And besides, it's none of her business. Why does Derrick have to tell her everything? And when did they have time to talk? Is that who she was talking to on the phone? And if so, why hasn't Derrick called *me*?

"Thanks," I say tightly.

"So are you going to come to my party tonight?" she says. "You totally have to. It's going to be so fun. We'll drink in my room, then maybe move it down to the beach?"

"Sure," I say. "Sounds great."

"Good." Her phone rings again, and she looks down at the screen. "I have to take this. Text me later." She turns and walks away, her hair bouncing behind her.

"You can come out now," I yell to Beckett once I see Juliana disappear down the sidewalk, heading back toward the hotel. "She's gone."

"Why didn't you tell her I was here?" he says. "Now if she finds out, she's going to know you lied."

"Because," I say. "She would have told Derrick. And she's not going to find out."

"But if Julia does find out—"

"Her name is Juliana," I say, rolling my eyes. "You really need to get better with names."

"I'm very good with names," he says as we step back out onto the sidewalk. The sun warms my skin, and I turn my face up toward the sky, enjoying the way the heat feels against my cheeks. "In case you haven't noticed, I have an amazing memory. I'm in all AP classes."

"It's impossible to be in all AP classes," I say. "The school only offers three of them. And you're not good with names, you don't even know mine."

"Of course I know your name," he says. "It's Pink."

"My *real* name," I say, even though I know he knows what I'm talking about.

He turns around in the middle of the sidewalk and stands in front of me, blocking me from moving forward. That same flush goes through me, the one that went through me this morning when he was standing so close to me near the car.

"I know your name," he says softly. "It's Lyla."

"You just know because you checked the tag of my suitcase," I say. I'm staring at his chest, because for some reason I don't want to look into his eyes. It's this weird unexplainable thing, like if I look into his eyes something . . . unstoppable is going to happen. Not that looking at his chest is much better. It's hard and muscular and I can't help but imagine what it would be like to reach out and slide my hands up under his shirt.

"No," he says. His voice is still soft, and it's lost its usual cockiness. "I knew before that."

"Oh." I swallow. My heart is hammering in my chest. "Then why did you ask me what my name was?"

"Because I felt like messing with you." His voice is back to his normal, cocky tone, and just like that, the spell is broken. I shake my head, then move around him and keep walking.

"Oh, what, you're mad now?" he asks, following me.

"No," I say. "In order to be mad at someone, you have to actually care about what they think of you, or what they've done to you. And I don't. Besides, if I was going to be mad at you, it wouldn't be because you gave me some dumb nickname and pretended you didn't know who I was. It would be because you sent me that note on the plane and then almost got me in trouble with Juliana."

"You got yourself in trouble with Juliana. And besides, I thought you said she wasn't going to find out you were with me. In which case, there would be no trouble for me to get you into in the first place."

I feel like I'm on some kind of weird merry-go-round, like no matter what I do I can't get out of the Beckett vortex.

Admit that it's kind of fun.

My phone buzzes, and I reach down and pull it out of my purse.

Just an email.

From me . . . to me.

Before graduation, I will . . . *learn to trust.*

A memory bubbles up in my mind. Aven, Quinn, and me, standing on the beach with our phones out, scheduling our emails to be delivered on this day. Aven said something about how by the time we were seventeen, we might think the emails were stupid. Quinn didn't think we would, but even so, we decided to have them repeat. Every couple of hours, throughout the day. So we wouldn't be able to ignore them.

At the time, I thought it was so clever of us, and I had an image in my mind of seventeen-year-old me getting the emails at different points throughout the day, realizing how important it was for me to work on my trust issues and thanking fourteen-year-old me for being so clever. Now seventeen-year-old me doesn't want to thank fourteen-year-old me—she wants to go back in time and throttle her.

I've already figured out my trust issues, I try to tell the past me. *I'm fine. I have a boyfriend. I don't have issues with men.* If I had issues with men, I'd be with someone like Beckett. Someone unpredictable and crazy and unreliable.

"What's that?" Beckett asks, trying to look over my shoulder.

"Just an email." I shove my phone back in my purse.

"From who?"

"From . . ." Something tells me "myself" is going to sound a little crazy. Besides, the last thing I want to do is tell Beckett about my email from the past. Or my trust issues. Well, my *past* trust issues. "It was nothing," I say.

"Then why do you look so disturbed?"

"I'm not disturbed!" I shake my head, trying to clear my thoughts. "Look, can you just take me to Derrick?"

"Sure."

I follow him down the sidewalk, past the shops and boutiques, weaving in and out of tourists wearing Hawaiian shirts and sunblock.

I feel a little . . . unsettled somehow.

It's okay, I tell myself. *You'll feel better when you're with Derrick. You always do.*

Of course nothing with Beckett can be that easy, because he insists on stopping for an ice-cream cone.

"What kind do you want?" he asks when it's his turn in line. The ice-cream shop is near the end of Ocean Boulevard and is called Big Olaf. The line, of course, was out the door, but did that stop him? No. In fact, it just seemed to make him happier. "Must be a popular place," he said cheerily when he saw the huge crowd.

"I don't want any ice cream," I say haughtily. It's a lie, of course. I never don't want ice cream. Especially on a day like today, when the sun is shining and the sky is blue and you can smell the ocean breeze.

He gives me an incredulous look, like he's not buying it.

"A double-scoop Heath bar crunch on a sugar cone."

Beckett raises his eyebrows. "Impressive, Pink," he says,

before turning back to the counter. "Two double-scoop Heath bar crunch on sugar cones," he tells the girl taking our order.

A secret little thrill runs through my body at the fact that Beckett deemed my ice-cream order good enough to copy. Suddenly, I'm ravenous. Beckett passes me my cone, then pulls a napkin out of the dispenser and hands it to me.

"Thanks." I start to pull out my wallet. "How much do I owe you?" He waves me away.

"It's on me," he says.

"Oh." I'm not sure if that's really appropriate. I mean, how would Derrick feel if he knew some other guy was paying for my ice-cream cone? Probably he wouldn't be too thrilled. I think about how I would feel if the roles were reversed and I found out a girl paid for Derrick's ice cream. Or, even worse, that Derrick paid for a girl's ice cream.

"Oh, relax," Beckett says as he pushes his way through the throng of people and back out onto the street. "It doesn't mean anything. It was three dollars."

"Thanks. I haven't eaten anything all day. Well, besides the package of cookies on the plane." I take a lick of ice cream, closing my eyes in pleasure as the sweet creaminess hits my taste buds.

"That doesn't count."

"Of course it doesn't," I say, satisfied. Derrick and I always fight about that—whether you can say you haven't eaten all day if you've technically eaten something. I say you can, as long as you haven't had a whole meal. Derrick says you can't, because snacks are still food. Which technically I guess is right, but—

Wait a minute. Why am I thinking about disagreements Derrick and I have had? And why am I comparing him to Beckett? That unsettled feeling comes back into my stomach.

"Are we almost there?" I ask, suddenly anxious to bring this whole excursion to an end. This is really not how I should be spending my first day of vacation.

"Yes."

We fall into silence as we walk down the street, licking our ice-cream cones and dodging people on the sidewalk. The streets are busy, filled with families leaving the beach, people heading out for an early dinner, and older couples poking into the souvenir shops. When we've passed all the restaurants and bars and gotten to the end of the road, Beckett leads me across one of the main streets and into a tiny parking lot. There's a small sandy path at the end of it, and I follow Beckett as he starts toward it.

"Where are we going?" I ask.

And then I look up from my ice cream. The beach comes into full view in front of me and almost takes my breath away. That's how beautiful it is. This is not like the kind of beaches they have in the Northeast, like the rocky ones on

Cape Cod or in Maine. Here, the sand is pure and smooth and white, and it slides over my flip-flops and in between my toes, cool and perfect. The birds that swoop and slide in front of the bright-blue sky are exotic-looking, different from the gulls that populate the beaches back home. The ocean sparkles in the distance, the water a deep aqua, the sun shining as it bounces off the waves.

"Wow," I say. "It's gorgeous." I've never been much of a beach person, but now, suddenly, I want to stay here. I want to lay out my towel and take a nap with the sun shining down on me. I want to spread out trashy magazines and lather myself with sunscreen and walk along the water so I can taste the salt in the air.

"It is," Beckett agrees.

We both just stand there for a moment, taking in the scene.

"So is there, like, a restaurant or something on this beach?" I ask as we start walking again. I picture Derrick sitting out on a deck somewhere, eating crab cakes and French fries, his face already starting to get red from the sun. Derrick loves eating outside. Usually I'm not a fan—the wind always blows your napkins around and bugs end up in your food—but for this view, it would be worth it.

"I'm not sure," Beckett says.

He's walking faster now, navigating through the throng of people who have set up their towels on the sand. Which doesn't really make sense. Why would he be heading toward the water? If Derrick is at some restaurant around here, shouldn't we be walking *down* the beach, toward where he might be?

"You're not sure if there's a restaurant, or you're not sure where it is?"

"I'm not sure if there is one. Or where it is." He turns around and grins at me, and then keeps walking.

I frown and then pick up my pace to keep up with him. "But you said you were taking me to Derrick."

"No, I said I was going to show you where he was."

"Okay," I say, not sure what the difference is. "So then where is he?"

"On the beach." Beckett holds his arm out and swoops it around, like the beach is his own personal gift to me.

"Where?" I shade my hand from the sun and look around. But I don't see Derrick anywhere.

"I don't know." Beckett shrugs. "He said he was going to the beach with Lincoln. So he must be here somewhere."

"He must be here *somewhere*?" I look at him incredulously. "Are you kidding me? You said you knew where he was!"

"I do know where he is! He's on the beach."

"The beach is, like, four miles long!" I can't believe this. I followed him around all afternoon, let him buy me a stupid ice cream, and now . . . *nothing*. He's been messing with me this whole time.

"It won't take you that long to find him," Beckett says.

"It will take forever to find him!" I say. "Look at all these people."

"Oh, come on," he says, in that infuriatingly cocky way of his. "You can walk four miles. It won't take you that long. Just text him and tell him you're on the beach. I'm sure it will be fine."

"It *won't* be fine," I say, deciding to leave out the part about how Derrick hasn't been answering my texts.

Instead, I turn around and stomp off. But of course I can't really stomp, because it's hard to stomp on sand. So I sort of just . . . slink away. I expect Beckett to call after me, to tell me he was joking and that he does know where Derrick is after all. But he doesn't.

I walk back down the sandy path and through the tiny parking lot and back onto the main street. People walk by me, happy and tan, laughing and joking, enjoying their vacations. But I'm in no mood for any of it. I'm too angry. I mean, who *does* something like that? Who leads someone on a wild-goose chase while knowing the whole time that they're just messing around? What's the point?

Maybe he wanted to spend time with you. And you wanted to spend time with him, too.

I shake the thought out of my head.

I'm so mad at him I could scream.

But I'm also mad at myself.

I never should have trusted him.

My phone buzzes then. I look down.

Before graduation, I will . . . *learn to trust*.

Wow. Universe one, Lyla zero.

FIVE

"PLEASE TELL ME YOU DIDN'T USE ALL THE hot water," Quinn says. She comes out of the bathroom and looks at me accusingly, like using up all the hot water is akin to kidnapping a child or stealing someone's life savings. "Please tell me" is one of her favorite ways to start a sentence when she's looking for a way to blame someone for something.

I remember her, two years ago, standing in front of the school. The three of us raising our voices at one another, which was scary, because we never did that. On the rare occasions we had a disagreement, we'd sit down and work it out calmly. Aven forced us to—she was the peacemaker, the one who thought everything could always be figured out by talking. But before the yelling started that day, I remember Quinn saying, "Please tell me you're not mad about this."

But of course I was. I was so mad I couldn't even look

at them, couldn't stop myself from yelling. Aven looked shocked when we started, and even more shocked when she finally started yelling back.

"I didn't use all the hot water," I say to Quinn now. "I've been out of the shower for at least an hour."

"Right." She sniffs and then rolls her eyes, walking back into the bathroom and slamming the door behind her.

It's later that night, and I'm in my room getting ready for Juliana's party. I'm not really in the mood for a party—after I left Beckett on the beach, I texted Derrick again (okay, fine, three more times), but he never responded. In the two years that Derrick and I have been together, he has *never* acted like this. He's the perfect boyfriend. He doesn't just disappear. And yeah, I know he's mad at me for lying to him, but mad enough to blow me off all day? It doesn't make sense. Something must be going on with him. But what? I can't figure it out, and the more I try, the more anxiety I feel.

Anyway, I don't really want to go to the party, but I can't just bail. One, because Juliana's been texting me to make sure I'm going to show up, and two, because I'm sure Derrick's going to be there. Just because he's been MIA all day doesn't mean he'll blow Juliana off—he knows she'd go batshit crazy. I wonder what that means, that Derrick's willing to ignore me all day but that he's *not* willing to ignore Juliana. Is Beckett right? Is Juliana in love with Derrick? Is Derrick in love with Juliana?

My stomach is starting to ache.

Must. Not. Think. Negative. Thoughts.

It's going to be fine, I tell myself.

Once Derrick realizes I've done nothing wrong, once we've worked it out, we'll be fine. In fact, we'll be more than fine. We'll be, like, all worked up and ready to have makeup sex. Which is the hottest kind of sex you can have. Not that I've ever had makeup sex. Obviously. But still. How awesome would it be to have the hottest kind of sex you can have the very first time you have sex? There will probably be all kinds of passion and romance. Derrick will throw me down on the bed and kiss me all over before having his way with me. A thrill runs up my spine.

I think about the sexy underwear I packed just in case. A black thong and demi-cup bra.

"Why the hell didn't I pack that bustier?" I mutter just as Quinn comes out of the bathroom.

"Wow," she says. "Sounds like a personal problem."

I open my mouth to reply with some snappy retort, but then I stop. Quinn is standing in front of me wearing . . . an outfit that is definitely not Quinn. She has on a red-and-white-striped skirt that stops way above the knee, and a white tank top that plunges so far down in front I'm afraid her boobs are going to pop out. Her hair falls in long waves around her shoulders, her eyes are brushed with metallic shadow, and a kiss of blush highlights the tan she must have gotten today.

"What the hell are you wearing?" I blurt before I can stop myself.

"Seriously?" she says. "You're wishing for a bustier and you're questioning *my* fashion choices?" She leans over the dresser in the corner and studies herself in the mirror. I watch, fascinated, as she wipes away a tiny smudge of mascara from the corner of her eye, then reaches into her purse and pulls out a lipstick. She paints her lips in a dark red, then drops the lipstick back into her bag. Then she steps back and fluffs her hair.

"Um," I say. "Is everything okay?"

She turns around to check her butt out in the mirror, and my mouth drops. The gesture is just so . . . not Quinn. She's not into makeup and dressing up and looking . . . well, *hot*. It's not that Quinn isn't pretty. It's just the opposite, actually. She has this rich chestnut hair and blue eyes and fair skin and a few freckles sprinkled across her nose. She looks a lot like Kate Beckinsale. But Quinn has never been wrapped up in her looks. Sure, she'd do her hair and slap on some lip gloss, but when it came to getting all dolled up? No way.

"Everything's fine," she says. "Why do you ask?"

She pulls out some perfume and spritzes it all over her body. I'm surprised she knows the appropriate pulse points.

"Since when did you start wearing perfume?" I ask.

"Since, like, forever," she says. But it sounds like it's a

lie. She gives herself one last long look, then squares her shoulders and tilts her chin up, like she's trying to convince herself of something.

"Are you sure you're okay?" I ask again.

For a moment, a look of doubt passes over her face, like maybe she's not sure she is. She opens her mouth, about to say something. But then she shakes her head just a tiny bit, almost like she's telling herself not to do what she was just about to do.

"Don't wait up," she says. Then she turns and walks out of the room.

Well.

Whatever.

Quinn's not really my problem.

In fact, she's not my problem at all. But still. There's an uneasy feeling in my stomach. I get up and tiptoe over to the door and peek out. I watch as Quinn gets farther and farther down the hall before disappearing into the elevator. I have this weird urge . . . like I should follow her.

No, I tell myself. *You and Quinn aren't friends anymore. You and Quinn are . . . well, not enemies exactly, but definitely not the kind of non-enemy ex-friends who can just go around following each other and demanding answers.* Quinn is a grown woman. Well, a grown teenager. A grown teenager who can make her own choices. And yeah, it's a little weird that she's dressed so . . . provocatively. But honestly, I don't even know Quinn anymore. She could go gallivanting around like that every single day for all I know.

Still. Maybe I should follow her. I imagine myself confronting her in the lobby and demanding to know where she's going dressed like that. Maybe I'll even call her "young lady" and drag her upstairs. She'll resist at first but then she'll give in, and then she'll—

My phone buzzes.

Derrick! It's Derrick! Derrick is texting me!

But it's not Derrick.

Just my mom.

Hope you're having fun, honey!

Yup, I type back. *Best time ever!*

Predictably, she doesn't ask for details.

Whatever. I have bigger problems than my mom's absenteeism. I need to get to Juliana's party so I can show Derrick what he's been missing all day.

Now I just need to find something sexy to wear.

By the time I get down to Juliana's room, I'm feeling a lot more confident. I'm wearing a really cute red spaghetti-strap sundress with a flared skirt, and I touched up my pedicure and added beachy waves to my hair with my curling iron. I look very Florida. And very sexy.

I pull the top of my dress down in front just a little bit,

then arrange my hair the same way Quinn did back in our room. Then I paste a smile on my face (my smile is one of my best features) and knock on the door to Juliana's room.

It flies open.

"Girl!" Juliana squeals, then reaches out and gives me a huge hug. She smells like a mix of alcohol and cologne. Not that she's wearing cologne, but the inside of her room reeks of it, probably from all the guys who are packed in here. "Ohmigod, I'm so glad you came." She gives me a huge kiss on my cheek. Her lips are all wet and lipsticky. Gross.

"Oh, of course," I say, reaching up and wiping at my cheek. "You know I wouldn't miss it."

"This vacation is the best," she says, spreading her arms wide as if to show just how much she loves it. She twirls around and then falls down on her bed. The crop top she's wearing slides up a little, exposing the bottom of her stomach.

A guy I've never seen before leans down and kisses her belly button. Juliana giggles. She's definitely wasted.

I make my way to the cooler on the other side of the room. What I really want to do is look around for Derrick, but I don't want to be too obvious. I need to be calm, cool, and relaxed, not wild like some kind of crazy stalker girlfriend.

I survey the contents of the cooler. Ice, wine coolers, cans of Bud Light, a two-liter bottle of Sprite, and some cheap vodka.

I grab a wine cooler and take a sip.

I stand in the corner by the window, which is open just a little bit, probably to air out the smell of pot that's permeating the room.

"Do you want some, Lyla?" Rory Corbett asks me, holding out a joint.

"No, thanks," I say.

"You sure?" she presses.

"Yeah, I'm sure." I take a step away from her, because Rory's a talker. She sits next to me in math, and she's always going on and on about the stupidest things—the color she's painting her room, her new jeans, the drama at her part-time job at Abercrombie. I cannot get sucked into the Rory vortex. I need to keep my wits about me.

I run my eyes over the room, nice and slow, looking for Derrick.

"Ohmigod, Lyla," Juliana slurs, appearing beside me and pulling on my arm. "You have to be in our dance contest."

"Your dance contest?"

"Yes, it's like, a marathon," she says. "We just dance and dance and dance and then whoever is the best wins!"

"Oh, that sounds fun," I lie. My eyes are flicking over the crowd, trying to find Derrick. But I don't see him.

"Are we looking for Derrick?" Juliana asks. "Because he's not here." She looks at me solemnly. "I think you miss him."

"No, I don't . . . I mean, yes, I do miss him." I'm confused by what to tell her. That I do miss him? Or that I don't? I don't want her to feel sorry for me. I'm not sure why, but the idea bugs me. On the other hand, I know that whatever I say to her is going to get back to Derrick. I take another sip of my drink. It's berry flavored, and very disgusting.

"Don't worry," Juliana says solemnly. "I'm going to help you. I'm very good at physiotherapy."

"What?"

"Psycho, I mean." She hiccups. "I'm good at psychother-apy." Then she reaches over and pats me on the head, like I'm a dog. "I'm going to help you both get through this trying time."

Her phone buzzes then, and she squints at the screen, try-ing to decipher a text. I let my eyes wander around the room, and tap my feet to the music that's blaring from someone's iPod. The lights in here aren't on, and it's kind of hard to see in just the fading daylight that's filtering through the windows.

In the other corner, a group of people are trying to play beer pong, which isn't working since there's only one small, circular table. I spot Aven standing by the entrance to the tiny kitchen, her arms crossed over her chest. She's talking to Liam, the guy she's secretly been in love with for, like, ever. They look like they're having a deep conversation, and I remember the way she cornered me at the airport, asking me if I was going to pay attention to the emails we sent ourselves.

Is she telling Liam she's in love with him? Is he going to reciprocate? I find it hard to believe that could really happen. I mean, they've been friends forever. If Liam had feelings for her, wouldn't he have told her? He doesn't seem like the kind of guy who would keep something like that a secret. Not that I know him that well—Aven always kept him sort of separate from us.

"It's Derrick!" Juliana crows. She throws her phone in my face. "He's going to stop back at his room and then be at my party in twenty minutes!" She waves the phone around, like I'm supposed to be reading the text, but obviously I can't. It's hard to read when she's so drunk and I'm so annoyed. Why is he texting Juliana before he's texting me?

"Don't worry," she says. "When he gets here, we'll have a session. You two need to work out your probbbbb-leeemmmsss." Her voice is getting louder as she talks.

"Sounds great!" I lie. "Be right back. I'm just going to run to the bathroom."

She doesn't hear me. Instead, she heads over to the iPod and starts fiddling with it, talking about her dance contest. Everyone is ignoring her.

I'm not going to the bathroom.

I'm going to Derrick's room.

I need to talk to him before he gets to the party. I need to work things out with him. And the last place I want to do it is in front of Juliana.

When I knock on the door of Derrick's room, a thumping noise comes from inside, like someone fell out of bed. It's probably Derrick. He has big feet. Maybe he's running to the door because he thinks there's a chance it might be me and he's so excited. Thank god he's on the first floor, otherwise whoever is below him probably would have called the front desk. Which is probably going to happen to Juliana's party at any minute. Maybe that's why she was in such a rush to get drunk. She knew she was on borrowed time. The school was very clear that we had to keep the peace and that if the hotel got any sort of—

The door flies open.

"Hiiii!" I trill. It starts off as flirty, just like I'd practiced in my head, and then sort of trails off into horror.

"Hiiiii yourself," Beckett says. He puts one arm up against the side of the door, blocking my view of the room. "Miss me already?" His eyes flick down to my chest, and I reach down and pull my dress back up.

"No," I say haughtily. Goose bumps have broken out on my skin. "I'm here to see Derrick."

"Derrick who?"

I roll my eyes. "Can you please just get him?"

"Fine." He turns around and yells, "Derrick! You have a visitor!" He turns back to me and frowns. "Derrick?" he tries again. "Derrick?" He smiles. "Oh, right. He's not here."

I take in a deep breath and resist the urge to scream. Why does he feel the need to mess with me like that? And for the second time today!

"You're not funny." It wouldn't be worth it to yell at him. That's what he wants. He wants to see that he's getting some kind of reaction from me. He wants me to get all worked up and wild. Well! He has another thing coming. I am certainly capable of controlling myself.

"You're welcome to come in and wait." He steps back and opens the door. "Of course, I'm not sure how long he's going to be." He tilts his head, pretending to consider it. "Are you?"

"Yes, I know how long he's going to be," I say. "He'll be here any minute. And if you think I'm going to come into your hotel room and wait with you, then you're crazy." I look around wildly for someplace else to wait, but of course there isn't one. I'm in a hotel hallway.

But there's no way I'm going into that room. I sit down on the floor, trying not to think about how many disgusting feet have walked over this carpet. It actually looks pretty clean, but you can never tell what kind of hidden bacteria could be lurking under the surface. They're always doing investigative reports on the dangerous germs that are all over hotels. Not thinking about that now, though, la, la, la.

I pull my phone out and send Derrick a quick text, telling him I'm waiting for him outside his room. I make sure to say I'm outside. The last thing I want is for Derrick to think I'm inside with Beckett. Shudder.

"Letting him know you're here?" Beckett asks conversationally. He slides down the wall until he's sitting right next to me.

"No," I lie.

"Okay." He shrugs.

I wait for him to say something smarmy, but he doesn't. He just sits there, his legs out in front of him all casual, like it's perfectly okay for him to be here next to me, even though he knows I hate him. Actually, I don't hate him. To hate him I'd have to actually have an opinion about him. And I don't.

All I know is that I'm here to see Derrick. *My boyfriend.* I have a right to wait for him. It's my right as, like, a citizen. Or a girlfriend. Or a patron of this hotel. The hallways are, like, common areas. To be enjoyed by all.

Beckett starts humming a little tune next to me, and I take in a deep breath, holding it in for one two three, then letting it out for one two three.

"Are you doing those breathing exercises we learned in yoga?" he asks.

"No."

"Yes, you are."

"No, I'm not." I reach into my purse and look around for something to keep my hands busy. But I don't have anything except makeup, and the last thing I want to do is put on lip gloss or something in front of Beckett. I don't know why, but it seems too . . . intimate.

He turns toward me, and his eyes move over my body. "You look nice."

I study his face for any traces of sarcasm. Wow. I forgot how green his eyes are. That same ripple of something (attraction? I don't even want to think the word ohplease-godno) goes skittering through my body. Only this time there's something more there. Something almost . . . *anticipatory*. It's weird. And unsettling.

I shift my leg away from his.

"When someone pays you a compliment, you're supposed to say thank you."

"Thank you." Where the hell is Derrick?

"So are you still mad at me then?"

Yes. "No."

"Are you sure?"

"Beckett, I don't even know you. How can I be mad at you?"

"You seemed pretty mad earlier."

"I wasn't."

"Okay."

"Okay."

We sit there for a few seconds in silence. My leg starts jittering up and down, and it takes all my willpower to get it to stop. The last thing I want is for him to think he's making me nervous.

"So is this"—he gestures to my hair and outfit—"all

for Derrick? Or were you planning on going out with your friend?"

"My friend?"

"Yeah. Quinn. I passed her in the lobby on my way in. She was decked out, head to toe." He grins, remembering. "Although she was wearing a lot less clothes than you are."

Something akin to jealousy hits my heart. Which is stupid. I'm not jealous of Quinn. "Quinn's not my friend," I say.

He shrugs. "Whatever."

And then he does something totally unexpected. Something totally crazy and weird and thrilling all at once. He reaches out and grabs my wrist, turns it over, and looks at the bracelet I'm wearing. It's just a bracelet . . . brown beads with a stretchy band. Nothing special. He runs a finger over one of the beads, tracing his fingertip along the swirly pattern of the different shades of brown and yellow.

"What's it mean?" he asks.

"What?" I'm startled. I've worn this bracelet every single day pretty much for over two years. Every. Single. Day. It's not an expensive bracelet. You'd think I would have lost it, or dropped it, or left it somewhere. In all this time of having it, someone should have stolen it, or it should have slipped off during gym, or it should have snapped off while I was doing something mundane like my laundry.

But it hasn't.

It's still on my wrist.

"What does your bracelet mean?"

"It doesn't mean anything." My breath catches in my chest.

"It's tigereye, right?"

I nod, still not breathing.

"So it must mean something." He turns my wrist over, inspecting the bracelet, then looks at me again, those eyes boring into mine. "So?"

"So what?"

"So what does your bracelet mean?"

"It's just . . . it's something I had with my dad."

"The tigereye thing?"

"Yeah."

He nods, thoughtful. His fingers have slipped off the beads now and onto my wrist, and his touch sends hot waves of sensation burning through my body.

I don't want to talk about my dad. I don't want to talk about him because I can't think about my dad without thinking about a million other things that could be upsetting—my mom, Quinn, Aven . . . they're all connected. Besides, my dad doesn't occupy any place in my life. He doesn't affect me. He's gone.

"He's gone?" Beckett asks, like he's reading my thoughts. I nod.

He tilts his head, looking thoughtful, his index finger still making lazy circles on the inside of my wrist. I know I should pull away, but I can't. It's mesmerizing, almost like he's put me in some kind of trance.

"Where did he go?"

"I have no idea." It's a half-truth. I don't know *exactly* where my dad is, but I do know he's in New Hampshire, living alone. Which makes it worse when you think about it—he didn't even ditch us for some other family. He just . . . left. And never bothered to contact us.

Because you betrayed him. You lied to him.

It all blooms up in my chest—the conversations with my dad, telling Aven about them, Aven telling Quinn, Quinn telling her mom, Quinn's mom telling my mom.

My mom, standing in front of me in the middle of the kitchen. *Is it true, Lyla? Are you leaving with him?*

"Lie." Beckett's still making circles on my wrist.

"He's in New Hampshire," I say. "He divorced my mom. He wanted me to go with him."

I take my hand away because I can't stand the way he's making me feel. Tingles and fireworks are flying all over, my heart is pounding in my chest, and my stomach is tangled.

I tell myself that the way I'm feeling doesn't have anything to do with Beckett. It's because I'm talking about my dad. And even if it was about Beckett, it doesn't mean anything. It's just . . . it's like looking at a picture of Channing Tatum or something. Which isn't cheating. Of course, Channing Tatum isn't here, rubbing my wrist while he asks me personal questions about my dad.

I scoot over a little bit on the rug, putting more distance between me and Beckett. But I still feel kind of warm, so finally, I stand up.

"Look," I say, "I'm not . . . I don't want to sit here and talk to you about my dad."

He doesn't even have the decency to be offended, like a normal person. Instead, he seems totally unfazed. "Okay," he says. "I figured."

"What's that supposed to mean?"

"Just that I assumed you wouldn't want to talk about your dad."

"Why? Because you're a total stranger who's been pretty mean to me?"

"No. Because it's obviously a sore subject for you. Which is too bad, because I'm a really good listener."

I snort. "I doubt it."

"Dare you to find out." His voice, just a second ago flirty and teasing, has turned kind of dark and smoky and all . . . I don't know, smoldering and husky.

His eyes rake up my body, starting at my legs and drifting all the way up until he's looking right into my eyes. It's so sexy I can hardly take it. I want him to like what he sees. Does he? He kind of seems like he does. His eyes have gotten all lidded and heavy, and he's staring at me from under his superlong lashes.

Dare you.

That's what he said. Dare you to find out. The words reverberate in my head, and with the way he's looking at me, I wonder if he's talking about my dad, or something else.

"What's going on?" a stern voice echoes through the hallway.

Derrick strides toward us, his eyebrows knitted together in a frown.

"Derrick!" I yell wildly. "It's Derrick! Hi, Derrick!" I gallop down the hall and throw my arms around him. "I missed you!" I give him a kiss, realizing too late that I probably don't want him to think I'm super excited to see him after he pretty much blew me off all day. I mean, shouldn't there be consequences?

"What's going on here?" he asks again, pulling my arms from around his neck.

"Nothing." Beckett stands up and shrugs. "I was just sitting out here getting some air, and Lyla came looking for you." He stretches his arms over his head, like he's exhausted and bored, and like he wasn't just undressing me with his eyes a few seconds ago. I can't decide if I'm disappointed that he's acting like it was nothing, or thankful he's not making a big deal of it in front of Derrick.

"Yup," I say. "It was nothing. We were just . . . I mean, I was just waiting for you."

Derrick glares at Beckett.

Beckett doesn't seem to mind. In fact, he seems to kind

of enjoy that Derrick's all suspicious. He gives him a big grin and then claps him on the shoulder.

"Well," he says, "I'll give you two lovebirds some time alone." He pulls a pair of sunglasses out of his pocket and puts them on, which is completely ridiculous since it's nighttime. "I have a party to go to."

"What party?" I ask, wondering if he's going to be at Juliana's, if I'm going to see him again in a few minutes. Derrick shoots me a look. "I mean, have fun!" I yell after Beckett as he starts toward the elevator.

I turn back to Derrick, and instantly, my heart squeezes. This whole thing with Beckett is so *stupid*. Derrick and I have been together for two years. Derrick is the one who's listened to me every time I complained about my mom's craziness. Derrick is the one who took care of me when the norovirus was going around our school and I couldn't keep anything down except Gatorade and dry toast. Derrick is the one who asked me to the junior prom by writing *LYLA, WILL YOU GO TO THE PROM WITH ME?* in rose petals all over my driveway.

Derrick is beautiful and perfect, and until today we've never even been in a fight. Well. Unless you count the time that he was visiting his family on the Cape for Thanksgiving and he told me he'd call me when he left at nine and then he didn't call me or text me until, like, midnight and I was mad because I'd thought he'd been killed in some kind of horrible fiery crash.

But even that was way back when we first got together. Since then, we haven't been in any other fights. He's been perfect. *We've* been perfect.

"I want to forget about today," I say, wrapping my arms around him again and inhaling his scent. He smells like sunscreen and the beach. I wonder why he smells like fun while all I've done all day is be miserable.

His shoulders stiffen for a moment, and I'm afraid he's still mad. But after another moment, I feel him relax. "I'm sorry I got so mad," he says. "I just got upset." He sighs. "I know you would never do anything to hurt me." He kisses me softly on the lips.

"I wouldn't!" I say. "I would never do anything to hurt you. Or us."

"Want to go walk on the beach?" he asks. His hands intertwine with mine.

"Yes," I breathe, thankful he's not suggesting going to Juliana's party. He wants to be alone with me! He can't be too mad then, right?

A fight. A walk on the beach. Moonlight. Racing hormones. I can't think of a better setup for what's about to happen. Sex. Sex. Sex. And lots more sex.

The beach is perfect. We sit at an outdoor restaurant, pigging out on nachos and potato skins, then order ginger ales to go. We pour half of the soda out of our plastic take-out cups and add wine from a bottle Derrick bought earlier using Lincoln's fake ID. We sip it while we walk on the beach, tipsy and happy, making jokes and giggling.

"I wonder what would happen if I just walked into the water," I say.

"You'd drown," Derrick says. "You're tipsy." He's smiling, but I feel like I can hear a little bit of disapproval in his voice.

"I'm not tipsy," I say, then immediately stumble in the sand. "Ooof." I giggle. *It's not my fault,* I want to say. *I'm wearing high heels.*

"You *are* tipsy," he says. "It's okay, though."

I know it's okay, I want to say. You're the one who gave me the wine and I've only had a little bit and there's nothing wrong with being a little tipsy it's Florida and it's vacation and what's the big deal especially because I know for a fact you were getting upset a few days ago because you couldn't figure out a way to bring pot on the plane. But I don't say any of that. Instead, I just take his hand and keep walking.

A few seconds later, he says, "Are you mad?"

"No." I push aside my annoyance. We're just getting back to being good. I'm not going to ruin even more of our vacation with another fight.

"Good." He stops and pulls me toward him, then tilts my chin up and looks at me. "I'm so sorry I took off earlier," he says. He runs his fingers down over my bare arms, then rests his forehead against mine. "I was just being a baby."

"No, you weren't being a baby," I say. "I shouldn't have let Beckett drive me to the airport. It was inappropriate."

"It's okay," Derrick murmurs. "You didn't have a choice."

But you did have a choice about sitting in the hallway with him and telling him about your bracelet and letting him stroke your wrist and getting all turned on while he did it.

I push my lips against Derrick's, trying to force myself to get lost in his kiss. I wrap my arms around his neck as the kiss gets deeper and deeper. After a few moments, he pulls away, breathless.

"Come on," he says. "Let's go back to your room."

SIX

WHEN SOMEONE INVITES THEMSELVES BACK to your room after you've just been passionately kissing under the moonlight, you kind of figure that maybe probably you're going to have sex. Especially if you've been talking about it for a whole day. Especially if Quinn and Aven aren't in the room.

And at first, it definitely seems like things are heading in that direction.

Derrick and I start to kiss.

Derrick and I kiss more.

Derrick's hands roam over my clothes.

We get under the covers.

My dress comes off. His shirt comes off.

So far we're not in new territory—we've been doing "everything but" for at least a year.

And that's when things sort of . . . stall out.

We're still kissing. We're still touching. But nothing's *progressing*.

I think about giving it a good swift nudge in the right direction, but I don't want to have to be the one to get this thing going, if you know what I mean. I grind my hips into his, hoping he'll get the message. The message being that he should take all my clothes off. I wonder if he's going slow because he's worried about me.

"Do you have a condom?" I breathe into his ear. Not the sexiest of segues, but we need to talk about safe sex! No way I'm going to be doing it without using a condom. I'm not on the pill, and the last thing I want is a little Dyla (Derrick and Lyla, get it?) running around. Oh, god. Now I'm going to have to get on the pill. I'm going to have to tell my mom, and she's probably going to get all weird and freak out and read, like, five million books about setting your daughter up to have a healthy view of sexual relationships. What are the laws for being under eighteen and getting birth control? Maybe I can just get some before I go, bring it back on the plane with me. Probably not, though. I have a feeling things are tighter here in Florida than they are in the Northeast.

"Um, yeah," Derrick says. "I have a condom."

"You do?" I'm surprised. Why would Derrick have condoms? Unless he bought them today when he was out.

"Yeah," he says. "I always have one. You know, just in case."

"Just in case what?" I'm trying to sound nonchalant, but I really have to make sure he means just in case I decide I want to do it, not just in case he runs into some random girl. Not that Derrick would ever cheat on me. Like I said, before today we haven't even been in a fight.

"Just in case you decide you're ready."

"Oh." I wonder how long he's had that condom. "It's not, like, expired, is it?" How horrible would that be? Being all responsible and then ending up pregnant or with an STD just because the condom was expired.

"No." He kisses my neck. Then my collarbone. Then my cleavage. I wait for him to keep going, to maybe kiss down my stomach and/or maybe take my bra off. But he doesn't do either of those things.

In fact, he stays right around my neck.

"Is everything okay?" I ask.

"Yeah," he says. "Everything's fine. Why?"

"Well, it's just that we're supposed to be having sex, and well . . . we're not."

"Oh. I didn't . . . I mean, I know you said you're ready, but I just want . . . I want to make sure this is really what you want."

"Oh, I want it." I do. At least, intellectually I do. My body is . . . I mean, I'm liking the kissing and everything, but I'm not . . . okay, fine. I'm not as crazy and excited as I was getting when Beckett was running his finger over my wrist like that. Not that it means anything. Of course I'm going to feel that way with Beckett. Beckett is dangerous and forbidden and makes my stupid hormones think they're in charge. Derrick is safe and amazing and perfect. Derrick is *better*.

I kiss his nose.

"It's just that you *just* decided this morning that you wanted to have sex," Derrick says. "And then we had kind of a weird day, and so I'm just wondering if maybe we should sleep on it."

"Sleep on it?"

"Yeah. You know, to make sure." He kisses me softly on the lips, then pushes my hair back from my face. "I wouldn't want you to end up regretting it tomorrow."

"Why would I regret it tomorrow? I love you. We've been together for two years. One stupid fight doesn't change any of that."

"I know." He sighs. "It's just . . . it's a big deal, and I want to make sure everything is perfect." He grins. "I want to have candles and champagne and a fancy dinner. Not us fighting all day and some cheap watered-down wine followed by a quick tumble in your hotel bed."

Who said anything about a quick tumble? A wave of annoyance rises up inside me, and I do my best to quell it. Why should I be mad at Derrick just because he wants to make sure everything is special? He's right. My first time should be something amazing, something magical, with flowers and candles and all the other things he was talking about.

What we're doing right now is probably something Beckett would do.

Why are you thinking about Beckett?

"Okay," I say, "you're right."

"Good."

I figure the making out will continue. Just because we're not going to have sex doesn't mean we can't do anything but. Instead, Derrick turns over in bed and then takes my hand.

"I'm sleeping over," he says. His voice sounds suddenly sleepy, like he'd just been watching TV or something instead of making out with me.

"Okay," I say. We've slept in the same bed a couple of times before. Once when his parents were out of town, and once when we both went to a party and ended up falling asleep in a random room after making out for hours. He wasn't complaining then about everything having to be perfect.

I turn over and wait for Derrick to pull me close, or at least say something to make me feel better about what I can't help but feel is a rejection. But he doesn't, and a second later, he's breathing softly, letting me know he's asleep.

The doors to the balcony are open, but the screen is shut. Warm night air floats into the room, and I can hear the gentle sound of waves against the shore mixing with the sound of voices downstairs. It's still early enough that most of my classmates are probably out, walking on the boardwalk or hanging out on the beach or eating a late-night snack in one of the restaurants.

Suddenly, I feel angry that I'm here, in my room, while everyone else is out having fun. But then I tell myself I should be happy to be here with Derrick—even if we didn't have sex, we're still in love. I'm still the luckiest girl in the world. And I'll bet lots of my classmates would rather be inside with someone they love instead of out there fending off sloppy drunk guys looking for random hookups.

My phone buzzes loudly, and I reach down to shut it off before it wakes Derrick up.

Before graduation, I will . . . *learn to trust.*

I check the clock.

Five minutes until midnight.

Five minutes and then these stupid emails will stop for good.

I turn over in bed and close my eyes.

But I don't fall asleep for a long time.

SEVEN

KNOCK.

Knock.

Knock, knock.

Knock, knock, knock.

I groan and roll over in bed, wondering who would be knocking on my door at this insane hour of . . . oh. It's nine o'clock. Still. Nine o'clock is way too early to be knocking on someone's door when they're supposed to be on vacation. I sit up and blink blearily around the room.

Quinn's bed is empty, but in the corner, Aven's curled up on her cot, the blanket wrapped around her, her thumb in her mouth. I shake my head. I can't believe she's still sucking her thumb. Quinn and I always used to tell her it was going to ruin her teeth, that her parents spent all that money on braces and she went through all that trouble making sure she wore her headgear even though everyone was having tons of sleepovers that year, which meant she had to—

Knock, knock, knock.

The knocking is a little more insistent now, but it's still relatively quiet. I guess whoever it is has the wherewithal to know they should at least try to keep it down. It's probably one of the teachers, trying to do a head count or something. No way can I let them catch Derrick in here. Even though we didn't even do anything. Sigh. I turn over and decide to ignore it.

Knock, knock, knock.

They knocks are coming faster now, and staccato-like, almost like a really gentle woodpecker or something. Well. If a woodpecker was inside and trying to take a head count. Which I really doubt would happen.

The knocking stops for a moment, and then there's a loud whisper.

"Lyla!"

Oh my god. It's Beckett.

Beckett Cross is at my door. Is he crazy? Why would he think it was okay to show up here? Does he want to get his ass kicked? I wonder who would win in a fight between Beckett and Derrick. Derrick is taller. And he plays sports. So he probably has better cardio. But Beckett has broader shoulders. And he might fight dirty—he probably knows moves and stuff you can only learn on the street.

"Lyla!"

Oh, Jesus Christ.

I get out of bed and open the door.

"Finally," Beckett says, then shakes his head like he can't believe I've left him waiting out here this whole time, as if we had breakfast plans and he didn't just show up here out of nowhere, calling my name when he knows I have a boy in my bed. His eyes rake up my body, and I become aware of the fact that all I'm wearing is a tank top and a really tight pair of shorts. I put them on last night after Derrick fell asleep—it was too cold to sleep half-naked, and besides, it wasn't like we were alone. I knew Aven and Quinn were going to be coming back at some point.

"Rough night?" Beckett grins.

"No." I cross my arms over my chest, and hope he can't see anything. He looks remarkably put together for someone who was probably out gallivanting and getting into debauchery last night. His hair is messy, but he's wearing baggy khaki shorts and a navy-blue T-shirt and sneakers with no socks.

"What do you want?" I demand. "I'm busy." The quicker he gets out of here, the better. Aven and Derrick are both heavy sleepers, but eventually one of them is going to wake up.

"I wanted to see if maybe you wanted to get coffee."

"*What?*" Is he crazy? Of course I don't want to get coffee. *Yes, you do.* No, I don't. *Yes, you do.* No, I don't.

"Why not?"

"Because I have a boyfriend!" I shake my head. Why am I trying to reason with him? He's crazy. And you cannot reason with a crazy person. I decide to change my tactic. I step out into the hall and close the door behind me. "Look," I say. "I'm dealing with something here, so you have to go."

"*Dealing* with something?"

"Yes. My friend Quinn didn't come back last night, and I'm worried about her." It's only a half lie.

"Yeah, she went home with a guy last night," Beckett says. "I saw her getting into some dude's car."

My stomach drops into my shoes. "Getting into some guy's car?"

"Yeah, they were coming out of a bar. Or a club. One of those places on the main strip." Beckett takes my hand and tries to pull me toward him. "Come on," he says. "I saw where they went. I'll show you."

"Whoa, whoa, whoa," I say. "I'm not going anywhere with you." I wrench my hand out of his grasp.

"Why not?" he asks, seemingly shocked.

"First, because I fell for that yesterday, and I'm not going to be lured into your crazy games again. And second, Derrick's in my room, and if he catches you here, he's going to flip." I stick my chin out, determined. "And besides, Quinn and I . . . it's none of my business where she is." But even as I'm saying the words, I'm nervous. Why the hell would

Quinn get into a car with some random guy?

Beckett just stares at me for a moment, not saying anything. It's actually a little bit uncomfortable, if you want to know the truth. Finally, just as I'm about to turn around and head back into the room, he speaks. "First of all, I'm not trying to lure you anywhere. I'm asking you to come with me. And second of all, if you think I give a shit about your douche-bag boyfriend, you're wrong."

"He's not a douche bag!"

"He is a douche bag. He didn't answer his phone after you missed the bus, he left you stranded all day yesterday, and then last night he made you wait at his hotel room while he took his sweet time." While Beckett's been talking, he's been walking closer to me, until the distance between us is almost nonexistent. "So like I said, he's a douche bag. And like I also said, I don't care about him."

"Whatever," I say. "I don't have time for this. Don't come to my room again."

I turn around and start walking back inside, hoping that Aven and Derrick slept through all that.

"She could be in trouble," Beckett calls after me.

I stop. But I don't turn around. "What do you mean?"

"Quinn. She might be in trouble."

I turn around. "I'm sure she's fine." Still, as I'm saying the words, an image of Quinn from last night pops into my head. That outfit. The way she was tossing her hair all around. The red lipstick. The way she walked as she left the room, like she was on a mission. "And besides, we're not . . . we're not really friends anymore." But I don't move.

"So? Aren't you the least bit worried about her?" Beckett asks. Then he shakes his head, like he's frustrated. "This is ridiculous. I'll take care of it myself."

He turns around and starts to walk away from me, back down the hallway toward the elevators.

"Wait!" I say. "You can't just . . . what are you going to do?"

He shrugs. "I'm going to make sure she's okay."

"How?"

"I saw the car she got into, and the neighborhood she was headed for. I'm going to go there."

"To check on her?"

"Yes."

"But you don't even know her." At least, I don't think he does. I don't remember Quinn ever mentioning or having any kind of interactions with Beckett. In fact, he's the exact kind of guy she hates. The kind who just shows up in class, doesn't take notes, and somehow still gets good grades. Quinn works hard for her grades. Really hard. And she doesn't like people who don't.

"So?" Beckett asks. "She might be in trouble. And if you're not going to do anything about it . . ." He trails off, like he can't believe I wouldn't want to do something to save Quinn.

"I'm sure she's fine. She probably just met a guy she wanted to hook up with."

Even as I'm saying the words, they don't sound right. Quinn, hooking up with some guy she just met? Quinn has only hooked up with one guy that I know of, and that was after she completely overanalyzed it and made a list of all the pros and cons. It was like a two-month-long process. By the end of it, the guy almost didn't even want to hook up with her anymore. Granted, it's been a while since we talked, but I have a hard time believing Quinn's changed that much.

Quinn, what is going on with you?

"Whatever," Beckett says, shaking his head. "Later."

I watch him start to walk down the hallway, and before I can stop myself, I'm calling after him, "Wait!"

He turns but keeps walking backward.

"I'm coming with you. Just let me grab a sweatshirt."

I tiptoe back into the room, shutting the door carefully behind me. Aven and Derrick are both still sleeping soundly. Aven's curly hair is poking out of the blanket cocoon she's fashioned for herself, and Derrick is now sprawled across the whole bed, snoring loudly.

I think about waking him up. I could ask him to come with me. It would be the right thing to do. Much better than just walking out with Beckett and leaving Derrick here all alone on the second day of vacation. And yeah, I know he left me yesterday, but still. Two wrongs don't make a right.

On the other hand, I don't want to take the chance there's going to be drama between Derrick and Beckett. If those two get into it, then who knows what will happen to Quinn? She could end up locked up in some skeezy guy's basement for years and years and no one will know where she is until she claws her way out using a pair of scissors she made out of twist ties. Well. That probably wouldn't happen, since Beckett seems to know where she is. But still. Why take chances with things like that?

The hotel room door opens an inch. "Lyla," Beckett whispers. "I'm going. Are you coming or not?"

I take a deep breath, then quickly scrawl a note on the hotel notepad that's sitting on the desk.

Went out to get coffee—be back soon.

Before this weekend, I'd never lied to Derrick once.

And now I've done it twice in two days.

"Are you sure you saw them come down here?" I grumble fifteen minutes later. It feels like we've been walking forever. And what was at first a nice little stroll on the beach has turned into just . . . walking down rows of streets. Lots and lots of streets.

"Yes," Beckett says. "It was a black Range Rover, and they definitely turned into this neighborhood." He's walking next to me, and every so often, his arm brushes against mine. I keep moving over on the sidewalk, but there's only so far I can go. The only thing that's keeping me from totally losing it is the fact that I'm wearing long sleeves. If I were wearing short sleeves, if our arms were brushing against each other and his bare skin was on mine . . . I shiver, then wrap my arms around myself.

"You cold?" Beckett asks.

"No."

"You're shivering."

"No, I'm not."

He shrugs. Even the way he shrugs is kind of sexy. I try to think of things to distract myself. The beautiful sun beating down on my face. The way the air is warm and perfect, not too hot, not too cold. The grit of the sand in my toes. The way this sweatshirt smells like Derrick. Yes, Derrick! Think of Derrick! How nice it felt to sleep with his arms wrapped around me last night.

Well.

One arm, at least.

How I fit against him perfectly in bed; how he was the big spoon and I was the little spoon.

How he didn't want to have sex with me.

No, no, no, do not think about how he didn't want

to have sex with me! Why didn't he want to have sex with me? It's definitely not because he doesn't want me. It's just because he wants to make it perfect. Because he's perfect. Tonight we'll have sex.

I wonder if I'll have time to shop for something really sexy. I'm kind of rethinking my black bra and underwear set. Maybe I should get something a little more . . . I don't know, trashy. But not trashy in a cheap way—trashy in a hot way. It should be sort of see-through, but not—

"There it is," Beckett says. He points to a one-story turquoise box house with a neatly manicured lawn. A shiny black Range Rover sits in front of it.

"Wow," I say. "She really looks like she's in a lot of trouble, Beckett. Thank god you got me out of bed to save her from this crack den."

He gives me a pointed look.

"What?" I ask.

"Well, aren't you going to go to the door?"

"Me?"

"Yeah, you."

"You're the one who saw her, why don't you go to the door?"

"Because I don't even know her."

"Yeah, but if I go to the door and she's been taken by some kind of gangster, then I'm going to be kidnapped, too."

I expect him to shake his head at my ridiculousness, but

instead he nods seriously, and his jaw sets into a line. "Good point. You stay here." He begins to march toward the door.

"Wait!" I call after him. But he's not listening. He's walking right up the driveway, all determined, like he has every right to be there. "Beckett, wait!"

He ignores me.

What the hell is he *doing*? Shouldn't we, like, have a plan or something? You can't just go marching onto people's property and banging on their doors, asking them if they're harboring a teenage girl in their basement. People don't like that.

I look around, wondering if I've missed anything that would lead me to believe this is a bad part of town. It doesn't look like a bad part of town. We're so close to the beach that I can still smell the ocean, and there's sand lining the road where the sidewalk meets the pavement. These houses have to be, like, millions of dollars. Okay, not millions. They're not mansions or anything. But I'll bet they're pretty expensive. My mom is always talking about how when you buy a house, it's all about location, location, location. And these houses are in a great location.

In fact, now that I think about it, it's very unlikely that Quinn has been kidnapped. Why would a kidnapper take her to some expensive almost-beachfront property? I've never heard of anything like that happening before. When people get kidnapped, they're always taken to some

run-down abandoned apartment building where the neighbors turn the other cheek.

This is definitely not that kind of neighborhood. This
is the kind of neighborhood where everyone knows everyone
else's business and everyone's worried about their property
values. In fact, even now as I'm glancing around there's a
woman across the street giving me the side eye. She's pretending to be watering her flowers, but she's not even
looking where the spray is going.

I give her a friendly smile, and she gives me one back, but
it can't hide her suspicion.

"Beckett!" I yell toward the front door. "Beckett, I think
we can go now!"

He turns around and looks at me, putting his hand up
to block the sun. "What?" he yells.

"I think we should go now! I think Quinn's all right!"
I shouldn't have said that last part. About Quinn being all
right. Now the neighbor woman's eyes are all wide, like I've
insinuated Quinn could be half-naked and tied up or something.

"It's okay," I say to her, hoping I sound and look responsible. I tug down my spandex shorts. "We're just visiting our
friend."

"Oh, that's nice," the woman calls back. She doesn't look
convinced.

I turn my gaze back to Beckett, who is now talking to some guy who's opened the door of the little turquoise house. Wow. The guy is seriously hot. He has messy dirty-blond hair and he's wearing black surfer shorts with no shirt. He steps out onto the porch, and his abs literally glint in the sunlight. His face doesn't look too happy, though. Probably because he can't figure out why some stranger has showed up at his house demanding to see Quinn.

"I just want to talk to her," Beckett's saying. Then he points to me. "See? That's her best friend right there, Lyla."

Oh, Jesus. Why did he have to get me involved? I don't even want to be here.

Now the hot surfer guy is staring at me. "You're Quinn's friend?" he yells across the street, looking confused.

"Yes!" Beckett says at the same time I say, "No!"

Beckett throws his hands up and gives me a *what the hell are you doing?* kind of look.

"I think she's okay," I say to Beckett. I turn and look at the woman with the hose, giving her another reassuring smile.

"Bill!" she calls toward her house. "Bill, I think you should come out here. And maybe get Harvey Cooper on the phone. That Flax boy is getting up to something again."

"No, no, no," I say. "No one's getting up to anything."

"Harvey Cooper is the president of the homeowners'

association," the woman reports. "And he's not going to be too pleased about being called back here for the second time in a week."

The second time in a week? Yikes. Well, even if Quinn's not in any danger, she better be careful about this alleged Flax boy. He sounds like trouble. He's probably always bringing tons of girls home and getting noise complaints. Someone that good-looking is definitely bad news.

I turn back to the house to call for Beckett again, but at that moment, Quinn emerges onto the porch. She's traded the outfit she was wearing last night for a pair of gray sweatpants and a navy-blue T-shirt that's about ten sizes too big for her. Probably that Flax boy's. Which means . . . wow. Did Quinn sleep with him? Well, if she didn't, they definitely did something. Her hair is all disheveled, and if I was closer, I bet I'd see that her makeup was a little smudged.

I peer at her, trying to figure out if she's been having sex all night. *Stop being so naive, Lyla,* I tell myself. Of course she's been having sex all night. She didn't just go home with some guy and end up in his clothes because they were studying together.

"Lyla?" Quinn yells once she sees me standing on the sidewalk. Her voice is a mixture of annoyance and confusion.

"Oh, hi," I say lamely.

"What are you *doing* here?"

"Just, um . . ." I glance around, looking for an excuse

as to why I would be here at this time of day, at this exact house, that would have nothing to do with her.

"We came to check on you," Beckett says. "Lyla, tell her we came to check on her!"

"Check on her for what?" the Flax boy asks. His tone is all dark, like he doesn't like anyone insinuating that maybe he's up to no good. Probably he gets up to no good on a regular basis, and so he's sick of people calling him on it.

"To make sure she was okay!" Beckett says. He turns to Quinn. "Quinn, are you okay?"

"Yes," she says to Beckett. She crosses her arms over her chest and glares at me. "I'm fine."

She seems really upset.

"You seem upset," I call to them from the end of the driveway. "We should probably go."

"Are you sure you're okay?" Beckett asks Quinn again.

"She's *fine*," the Flax boy says. "Now you want to tell me who the hell you are and what the hell you're doing here?"

"Jesus," Beckett says. "Take a chill pill. We're friends of Quinn's. We just came to make sure she was okay. Which we already told you."

"Quinn, are these people friends of yours?" the Flax boy asks her.

"No," Quinn says, surprising everyone. Even the Flax boy looks a little surprised, like up until she said that, he thought he was making a big deal out of nothing.

"Bill!" the woman across the street yells. She drops the hose, and a river of water goes snaking down her grass. Those flowers are definitely going to be ruined now—she's going to end up drowning them if she keeps carrying on like that. "Bill, come quick! There's going to be a domestic disturbance!"

"No there's not," I yell after her. I turn back to the driveway. "Beckett! Come on! She's fine! Let's go!"

Beckett shakes his head one more time at the Flax boy, like he can't believe how stupid he's being. Like the Flax boy should be happy that he took Quinn home to hook up and then had a bunch of strangers show up on his doorstep to question his motives and get the neighbors all riled up. Then he turns around and walks back toward me.

"That guy's an asshole," he says as he walks down the driveway.

"Shh!" I say.

But it's too late. The Flax boy heard him. "Hey," he calls after Beckett. "What'd you call me?"

Beckett turns around. "I called you an asshole," he says.

The Flax boy's eyes darken. He's very sexy when he gets all smoldery like that. I'm sorry, but I can kind of see why Quinn would want to go home with him. I mean, if you had to pick a boy to have as your vacation hookup, this guy is exactly what you'd want.

I look at Quinn. She's standing on the porch, looking a little dazed. Is she really okay? I wonder. I give her a smile, but she scowls at me and looks away. All righty then. She must be at least a little bit okay. I really doubt someone who was being held against their will and tortured would be so unfriendly, even to an ex-best friend.

Then her eyes suddenly widen. "Are those my shorts?" she calls.

"No," I say hotly. "They're mine." These shorts are just plain black shorts. She's not the only one who can wear plain black shorts. Everyone has a right to them. They're, like, in the public domain.

"What did you call me?" the Flax boy asks again, like it's so unbelievable he needs to hear it twice.

"I. Called. You. An. Asshole." Beckett moves closer, and I reach out and grab his arm.

"Bill, the police, call the police!" the woman across the street screams.

"Come on," I say to Beckett, "this isn't any of our business."

"Get out of here," the Flax boy says to us.

Beckett takes a step toward him, like he's going to completely disregard the fact that we're trespassing on someone else's property and that said person is pretty much threatening Beckett.

"Beckett!" I say. "Stop. Just stop."

In the distance, I hear the sounds of a siren.

"That's the police!" the woman yells from across the street. "My husband has called the police! And as soon as they get here, I'm going to fill out a report. I'm going to fill out a report and make sure that this neighborhood doesn't go the way of the ghetto!"

Wow. That is definitely not PC. I don't think you can really just walk around saying you don't want your neighborhood to go the way of the ghetto. I think you have to call bad neighborhoods "transitioning." Although it definitely doesn't pack the same punch to say you don't want your neighborhood to end up "transitioning."

"Beckett," I say, "please, come on."

He turns around and looks at me, and when he sees my face, it must snap him out of it. "The police are going to come and arrest you!" I yell, just to drive the point home. "Do you want to spend the day in *jail*?"

"Fine," he says, "come on." He starts to head down the driveway, but he's walking backward, still staring the Flax boy down. The Flax boy is staring him down, too. I have the feeling that if Quinn and I (and the neighbor woman) weren't here, then they'd probably have started fighting. How stupid. Boys and their dumb hormones. Who cares if we're here looking for Quinn? Why do they have to make a big deal about it and get all up in each other's faces? This isn't medieval times. Nothing has to be settled with force.

The sirens are getting louder. Can you imagine if I got arrested during my senior trip? I'll end up at some police station and have to get a mug shot taken. Actually, I don't know if they do mug shots if you're under eighteen. I don't even know if they arrest you if you're under eighteen. They might just send you off to juvenile hall. Not like that would be better—could you imagine my mom getting a phone call saying I was being sent to juvie? Talk about her anxiety kicking into high gear.

The sirens are getting louder and my heart is pounding and I can't take it anymore.

I grab Beckett's sleeve and yell, "Run!"

EIGHT

"ARE THEY COMING?" BECKETT ASKS A FEW
blocks later.

We're running at top speed and he's not even out of
breath. Me, on the other hand—my legs are on fire and my
chest feels like it's going to explode. I glance behind me. "I
don't know," I say. "I don't see anyone." I can't hear the sirens
anymore either. But they could have cut them off to lull us
into a false sense of security.

"Should we come up with a cover story?" Beckett asks.

I look at him in admiration. "Good idea," I huff. I hope
he's going to take the lead with that, since I don't think
there's any way I'm going to be able to come up with a good
story. I'm not that good at fiction. I wrote the worst stories
for creative writing. Luckily, it was an elective and didn't
really count for anything. I got to take it pass/fail. Plus, it's
not like I find myself in these situations all the time. I'll bet

anything Beckett is the one who's been in trouble with the cops a bunch. Probably that's why he and that Flax boy got into it. Troublemakers don't like when they come in to contact with other troublemakers. It becomes explosive.

But if Beckett's good at coming up with cover stories, he's not offering one.

"So?" I prompt.

"Maybe we should tell them we got an anonymous call that Quinn was being held against her will."

"That . . . doesn't . . . make . . . any . . . sense," I huff. For someone who's supposed to have a lot of practice at this, he's actually very bad at it. I can't take it anymore. I stop running and bend over and grab my knees while I catch my breath.

"Come on," Beckett says, jogging in place. "Hurry up! They're coming! The police are coming! We're going to end up in the clink!"

My anxiety skyrockets, then immediately comes crashing down when I get a look at his face. He looks kind of like he's laughing. Or about to. And then I get it. He's making fun of me.

"You're making fun of me," I say, stunned.

"No, no, I'm not. I really do think we should go running away from a police car that probably wasn't even coming for us."

I stare at him incredulously for a second, then turn and start walking. "You're a jerk," I say.

"Hey, hey, hey," he says, coming after me. "Relax."

"I will not relax!" I pull the sleeves of my sweatshirt down over my fingers and try to get a look at the street signs without Beckett noticing. I want to make sure I'm going the right way without actually letting him know that I'm looking to see if I'm going the right way. "You pulled me out of bed at seven in the morning because you told me Quinn was being led to a drug den."

"First of all, it was nine o'clock, and second of all, I said nothing about a drug den."

"Then," I say, starting to get going, "you almost got into a fight with a guy for no reason. Quinn wasn't in trouble; she was doing something totally normal!"

"Hooking up with that loser is definitely not normal."

"*Then* you got the police called on us and made fun of me when I showed the least bit of concern."

"True, if the least bit of concern is you freaking out and screaming at me to run."

"That's not—I don't—" I'm confused now. Should I be mad at him or not? We're getting close to the main part of town, the drag of Siesta Key, and I'm starting to feel a little silly. We weren't going to get hauled away to jail in the middle of the day. If anything, the police probably would have been questioning the guy Quinn was with, wondering why he had a girl with him and why we were concerned.

"Ooh, run, run, we're going to end up in the clink!"

Beckett says in a high-pitched voice, mocking me.

A couple of girls in bikinis walking by look at him and giggle, and I can't help but laugh, too. He looks ridiculous.

"I'm not the one who said anything about the clink." The air is starting to get a little warmer now, and I pull a hair tie off my wrist and gather my hair into a ponytail. "You said that."

"Yeah, well, I was just getting into the spirit of things." He kicks at a pebble that's on the ground.

"Well, good job."

He smiles at me. "Look, I'm sorry I came to your room like that and got you all worked up. I really just wanted to make sure Quinn was okay. But I guess I overreacted."

"Nah, it's fine," I say. "It was nice of you to look out for her."

He gives me a smile, and I feel like it's genuine. I remember last night, sitting with him outside his hotel room, the casual way he took my wrist and ran his fingers over my skin. I resist the urge to shiver. I also resist the wave of guilt that rises up inside of me when I think about letting him do something like that when I have a boyfriend.

Relax, I tell myself. *You couldn't have stopped it.* I mean, what would I have said? Beckett, don't ask me about my bracelet? I would have sounded like a crazy person.

"Let me make it up to you," Beckett says now.

"How?"

"With the one thing no one can resist."

"And what's that?" I ask, almost afraid of the answer. A flash of us in bed together, our legs tangled under the sheets, goes through my head.

Beckett grins and points at a little hut I never noticed before, even though it's on the main drag and I must have walked by it at least four times yesterday. It's a building really, or a stand, with a window in front where they serve people. Almost like an ice-cream truck, but they're not serving ice cream.

"Doughnuts," Beckett says. "The best ones, like, ever."

"How would you know?"

"What do you think I've been eating since I've been here?" He gives me a *duh* look, like of course he's been here eating doughnuts the whole time. It's so . . . I don't know, *normal* that it almost makes me a little uncomfortable. I don't like thinking of Beckett as a normal person with food preferences and dietary habits. It makes him seem too real, and as long as I keep thinking of him as a caricature, the better off I'll be. Up until now Beckett has been the hot guy who is fun to look at but is seriously trouble, who I would never jeopardize my relationship for. And that's how I want him to stay.

I glance at my watch: 10:07. I'm betting Derrick won't be awake until at least eleven, and honestly, what's the harm in a little doughnut?

"Sure," I say as my stomach rumbles in anticipation.

Beckett orders me a glazed without asking what I want, promising me it will be the best doughnut I've ever had. We get plastic cups full of freshly squeezed orange juice and wrap our warm doughnuts in napkins so we can eat them while we walk back to the hotel. The tourists are already out in full force, streaming toward the beach in wide lines, holding folding chairs and coolers and brightly colored towels. Everyone has the happy look of people who are on vacation.

When we reach the parking lot that leads to the beach, Beckett raises an eyebrow at me, asking if I want to continue. I nod, and we keep walking, our feet sliding into the cool white sand, so different from the beaches back home, where the sand is hot and sort of grainy.

"I still can't believe the sand is so cool," I say.

"They call it sugar sand," Beckett says.

I raise my eyebrows in surprise.

"What?" he says defensively when he sees the look I'm giving him. "I know things."

"Oh, yeah? Like what?" I can hear the flirting tone in my voice, and I blush and look back down at the sand, hoping he doesn't think I was flirting with him. Which I wasn't. I don't flirt with guys. Except Derrick. Not that we've been flirting much lately. Once you're in a relationship with someone, a lot of the flirting kind of stops.

"Lots of things. Like how Virginia is the state with the

highest population of elm trees and how the biggest ball of yarn is in Illinois."

"Yeah, well, did you know that the oldest railroad is in Pennsylvania? And that the first twenty-four-hour diner was in Minnesota?" I shoot back.

"Really?"

"No," I admit. "I just made all that up."

He grins. "Me too."

I reach out and push him playfully. "Jerk."

He doubles over, pretending that I hurt him. "Ooh," he says. "Remind me not to mess with you, McAfee. You're stronger than you look."

We are definitely flirting. Definitely. A weird feeling flows through my body, excitement mixed with fear mixed with anticipation. And guilt. I can't ignore the guilt. It's there, under the surface, threatening to take over.

"Wanna walk down by the water?" Beckett asks.

I want to. But I know I shouldn't. I should head back to the hotel, I should wake Derrick up, I should see what he wants to do today. I should start planning for the perfect day to go along with the perfect night.

Before graduation, I will . . . learn to trust.

The email pops into my head. I don't know why. They've finally stopped coming. I'm supposed to be free of them. I don't want to think about the email. But I am. And isn't part of learning to trust learning to trust yourself?

"Sure," I say. "Let's walk by the water."

The water is cold, but after a few minutes, my feet get used to it. The morning is like something out of a movie or a painting—birds swoop and swish across the sky, dipping their beaks into the water to hunt for their breakfast. It's early enough that the college kids aren't awake yet, and the beach is filled mostly with families and older couples. A little girl in a ruffled pink bathing suit toddles by and plops herself down, sticking a shovel into the wet sand and scooping it into a bright-yellow pail.

Beckett and I don't say anything for a few moments. We just keep walking, eating our doughnuts and drinking our orange juice.

"So what's the deal with you and Derrick?" Beckett asks once we hit a spot on the beach that's a little less crowded. He breaks off a piece of his doughnut and pops it in his mouth.

"What do you mean?"

"I mean, is it serious?"

"Of course. We've been together for two years."

"So what are your problems about?"

"We don't have any problems!" I say, shocked.

"Then why were you spending all day yesterday looking for him?"

"I wasn't. He was just mad because I lied to him about how I got to the airport."

"You told him your mom took you?"

I nod and take a small sip of my orange juice. Something about this feels wrong—talking about Derrick with Beckett. It feels like a betrayal. I heard once that if you feel weird about what you're doing in your relationship, you should imagine how you'd feel if your boyfriend were doing it—and if you'd be mad at him, then it's wrong. For example, I should think about Derrick being out here with another girl, buying her doughnuts and walking on the beach with her while I'm back at the hotel, sleeping in our bed. It fills me with fury just thinking about it. I would be pissed. I would never forgive him.

"Then why are you here with me now?" Beckett asks.

I think about it. "Because I want to be." It's a simple answer, but it's the truth.

"And do you always do everything you want?"

"Not really." The words are out of my mouth before I realize I'm saying them.

"Like what?"

"This conversation is stupid."

"Why? Because it's getting too close to talking about something real?"

The water's starting to feel cold again, and I take a few steps away from it, wriggling my toes in the sand. "Oh, now you want to talk about something real?" I ask.

"Why wouldn't I?"

We're coming up to the main part of the beach now, and he heads over to a trash can and throws away his empty orange juice cup.

"You don't seem like the kind of guy who's into having real talks."

"Really? I'm so into real talks. I'm the realest real, like, ever."

"Okay, fine," I say as we keep walking. "Tell me about why you're such a player."

"Excuse me?"

"Why you're always with a different girl," I say.

He looks shocked that I would insinuate such a thing.

"Oh, please," I say. "I've seen you in the halls at school."

"I don't know what you're talking about."

"That's what I thought," I say, sighing. "The realest real talker ever. Riiiighht."

"Okay, fine," he says. He takes in a deep breath and thinks about it. "I don't know," he says finally. "I guess I've never really thought about it."

"So think about it."

"I guess it's just . . . easier."

"Easier?"

"Yeah. As long as I don't get too close to someone, there are no expectations."

"What's wrong with expectations?"

He shrugs. "I get enough of that at home."

"Your parents put a lot of expectations on you?"

He nods.

"What sort?"

"Everything. School, sports, whatever. It's nice to have relationships where no one cares about what you're doing."

I roll my eyes. "They care about what you're doing, Beckett. You just leave before they can give you crap about it."

He opens his mouth to protest, then shuts it. "Yeah," he says, "you're probably right." He at least has the decency to look a little disturbed by this revelation. "So I told you something," he says. "Now you have to tell me something."

"Like?" Please don't ask me about Derrick, please don't ask me about Derrick.

Beckett reaches out and tweaks my bracelet. "This," he says.

"I told you, my dad gave it to me."

"And now he's gone."

"Yes."

"And yet you're still wearing it?"

I swallow. "Yes."

"So what's the deal with it?"

"I just . . ." I take in a deep breath, wondering how much

I should say. I haven't talked about the thing with my dad ever since my fight with Quinn and Aven.

I stop on the beach and look out across the water. The sun dances off the waves.

"I'm not . . . it's hard for me to talk about."

He nods but doesn't say anything.

"I told you how my dad left," I say. "How he decided to leave my mom. And how before he left, he asked me . . . he asked me to go with him."

"To New Hampshire."

I nod.

"And you told him no?"

"I told him I would think about it." The flash comes again. Me, telling Aven about how my dad wanted me to go with him. Telling her I was thinking about it, asking her not to tell anyone. Aven promising me she wouldn't, and then doing it anyway.

"But then you didn't?"

"No." I shake my head. "I decided to stay with my mom."

"And you and your dad . . ."

"He left the morning after I told him. And I haven't heard from him since."

Beckett nods, like he's thinking about it. I feel the familiar lump in my throat, the lump that comes every time I talk about my dad or think about my fight with Aven and Quinn.

Beckett stares straight ahead, and a seagull dips down and

lands in front of him. It picks at the sand, its thin little beak digging around for something to eat. "You know, seagulls get a bad rap," he says. "They're actually really pretty birds."

I wrinkle my nose. "Yeah, but they're so annoying."

"A lot of birds are annoying. But seagulls are always around—you see them all the time. So you forget how beautiful they are."

"I guess that's true." I play with the bracelet on my wrist, and the lump in my throat starts to loosen. I'm thankful he's not pushing me, not making me talk about it more. It's enough that I've said what I did.

We start walking again. There's a couple jogging in the other direction, and when they get close to us, we move a little bit toward the water, letting them pass. Beckett's arm bumps against mine at the same time my feet hit the water. I shriek as the tide hits my ankles. Beckett laughs, then stomps in the water, sending droplets flying everywhere, including onto my bare legs.

"Quit it!" I say, but I'm not mad. "It's freezing!"

"Ahh, don't be a wimp," he says. He wades into the ocean a few steps.

"Are you crazy?" I say. "It's too cold for that!" Getting your feet used to it is one thing. Wading is another.

"No, it's not." He splashes water on himself, but I can tell he's cold. "See? It's refreshing."

"Really?" I take a few steps into the water. It's freezing.

"Oh, you're right," I say, pretending to believe him. I step past him and shade my eyes from the sun. "Oh, look, there's a sandbar over there," I say. "Wanna walk to it?"

I turn around, catching the tail end of the look of panic that's crossing his face. I raise my eyebrows in what I hope is an innocent look. But it must not work, because a second later, he appears by my side.

"Oh, good idea," he says. "Let's go out to the sandbar."

"You first," I say.

"Oh, no, ladies first," he says, and makes a little gesture with his hand, like he's being chivalrous.

I take a couple of steps forward, telling myself it's easy. La, la, la, nothing to see here. I try to pretend the ocean is a huge Jacuzzi, and the waves are swirling around me, hot and soothing, making my muscles relax as I walk and warming me to the core. Step, step, step. See? It's fine. The water has actually stopped getting deeper now, and I'm kind of getting used to the cold. Why is the water so cold anyway? The sun is warm. The air is warm. So why wouldn't the water be warm? I try to remember the stuff we learned in ninth-grade earth science about temperature vectors and patterns.

Other people are swimming around in the water like it's nothing. A little boy a few yards away is splashing around happily, dunking himself under and then popping up, his hair dripping wet. A little farther out, a man is pulling a woman along on a boogie board.

So then why am I so cold? Do I just need to get more used to the water, or is there something wrong with me? Do I have a problem with my internal temperature? Of course, if I do, then Beckett does too, because—

"Ahhh!" Before I know what's happening, the sand gives out below my feet, and I'm suddenly up to my thighs in water. I turn back toward the shore, but I'm having a hard time getting my footing.

"Whoa, whoa, whoa," Beckett says, and then his arms are around my waist, steadying me. He pulls me back just a little bit, until my feet find the sand again. "You okay?"

"Yeah," I say, my heart pounding in my chest. "There was a drop."

"You sure you're okay?" His hands are still on my waist, holding me steady. And I'm glad, because suddenly my knees feel weak, like they could give way at any moment.

"Yes," I say. "I'm fine."

"That's really dangerous," he says. "I should talk to someone about that."

"Oh, please." I roll my eyes. "It's fine. It didn't even go up to my waist."

"Still. It could have wrecked your phone." He slips his index finger into the top of my shorts pocket and runs it over the edge of my phone.

"Well, thank god it didn't." I don't know how I'm able to talk. His hands are on my waist, and his face is so close to mine I'm afraid (hoping?) he's going to kiss me. He leaves his finger in my pocket, his eyes on mine. His tongue snakes out and licks his bottom lip, and it's the sexiest thing I've ever seen in my whole life.

He's hardly even touching me and I feel like I'm on fire.

"We should go back to the hotel." I say the words before I can decide if I mean them. My brain screams at me to stop saying things like that, that if I stop this moment and what might be about to happen, I'll never be able to get it back, I'll never be able to do something that I really, really want to do.

"Is that what you want? To go back to the hotel?" Beckett shuffles a little closer to me until his chest is pressed up against mine.

"Yes." My voice sounds weak.

"You sure?"

"Yes."

But he doesn't move.

Everything feels like it's moving in slow motion, and everything around us is suddenly magnified. The sound of the waves as they crash lazily against the shore. The brightness of the sky and the sun and the slash of white clouds against the horizon. It's like my every sense is on alert, and after a few more moments, I can't take it anymore. I close my eyes.

I'm not sure if Beckett thinks it's an invitation to kiss me. I'm not sure if I knew there was a chance he might and that's why I did it. But his lips brush against mine, slowly, slowly, slowly, so slow I'm not sure if it's even happening.

But then I feel his hands tighten around my waist, I feel him pull me closer and the water is so warm, it's like a huge warm bathtub and my muscles are all weak but it doesn't matter because he's holding me up and he's kissing me and oh my god it feels so good. The stubble on his chin is rough against my skin, but his fingers in my hair are soft and perfect.

He pulls away first, then looks me right in the eye. "Lyla," he breathes. No one has ever said my name like that. His voice is smoldering and sexy.

I swallow, trying to find my voice.

Derrick.

His name pops into my head, and I take a step away from Beckett. My heart is pounding in my chest, and I feel like the ground is spinning.

And that's when I see her.

Juliana.

She's standing on the beach, wearing a flowing white sundress with spaghetti straps. She's holding a big green beach bag in one hand and shading her eyes from the sun with the other. She purses her lips and then starts walking toward us.

"It's Juliana," I say dumbly. The sun and the ocean and the sand and the kiss are messing with my brain, making it hard to think.

Beckett sighs. But he doesn't look surprised that she's coming over here.

I start wading through the water toward the shore. Beckett follows me.

"Wait up," he says.

But I don't slow down. I can't believe I cheated on my boyfriend. I can't believe I got caught up in some ridiculous fantasy. I can't believe Juliana saw us. I can't believe I was so *stupid*.

"Lyla," Beckett calls. "Slow down." I'm walking fast, because the sand near the water is packed hard. As I move away from the ocean, the sand gets softer, and it's more difficult to keep my footing.

But I don't care.

I start to run.

And I don't stop until I'm back at the hotel.

NINE

I AM *REALLY* OUT OF SHAPE.

I mean, it can't be more than half a mile from where I was on the beach back to my room. And yet by the time I get to the hotel lobby, I'm sweating. I've probably run more today than I have in the past two years. Maybe even in my whole life. Well, besides when we have to run the mile in gym, but that doesn't really count. And actually, I never ran it last year because I made sure to be absent on that day. Go me.

When I get back to my room, I pause outside the door. Should I have run away like that? Maybe I should have tried to talk to Juliana, to explain to her that what she saw wasn't what she thought. Maybe I should have pretended to slap Beckett, to make it out like he kissed me and I hated it.

I shake my head. It's too late now. I can't go back to the beach. And now that I'm back here, I have to tell Derrick

what happened before Juliana does. I just hope he under-
stands. My eyes fill with tears, but I blink them back and
open the door to my room.

Derrick is still in bed. He's lying on his side with his pillow over his head. He looks so . . . sweet and innocent. He has
no idea that his girlfriend just cheated on him.

The tears in my eyes multiply. This is awful. This is more
than awful. How could I do such a thing? And right after
I told him he had nothing to worry about, that there was
nothing going on with me and Beckett. I blink even harder,
trying to make sure the tears don't spill over my cheeks.

"What's wrong?" a voice chirps from the other side of
the room.

I jump.

Oh. It's just Aven.

I forgot she was still in the room.

"Nothing's wrong," I say.

"You're getting that look on your face," she says.

"What look?"

"The look you always get when you're about to cry."

"I do not have that look on my face!" I think about it.
"And besides, I don't get a look on my face when I'm about
to cry."

"Yes, you do. Your bottom lip gets all wobbly and you
get these weird little wrinkles at the side of your eyes." She
tilts her head and looks at me, considering. "If you're going

to cry, you should probably just cry, because if you keep letting your face get wrinkled like that, you're probably going to need Botox when you're older."

I can't take it anymore. The tears start to fall over my cheeks.

"Oh, wow," Aven says. Her face softens, and she actually sounds really concerned. "Lyla, I'm sorry. I was just kidding. You're not going to need Botox when you're older. You have really nice skin."

"I'm not crying because of that," I say. "I just . . ." I'm trying to keep my voice down, but it's becoming harder and harder. If Derrick wakes up and sees me here, crying, he's going to ask why. And I have no good reason. Actually, I do have a good reason. Just one I'm not sure I'm ready to tell him.

I turn and rush back out of the room, and when I get in the hallway I lean against the wall, taking deep breaths and trying to calm myself down.

A second later I feel a hand on my back. Aven.

"What's wrong?" she asks.

I take in long, deep breaths. I feel like I'm going to hyperventilate. "I did something really bad to someone," I say. I'm not sure why I'm confiding in her. Maybe because the secret just feels too big to hold on to myself, too bad to completely sit with all on my own.

"Who?" she says.

"Derrick." I wipe my eyes and then slide my back down the wall until I'm sitting on the floor.

Aven nods seriously, like she knows all about it. "Stay here," she commands. She disappears down the hall and returns a second later holding two cans of Sprite and a king-size package of peanut butter cups.

She sits down on the floor next to me and hands me a soda.

"Thanks." I sniffle and pop the top, then take a sip of the cold fizzy liquid.

"You're welcome."

We don't say anything for a second, just sit there, both of us sipping quietly.

"So what did you do?" she asks finally.

I shake my head. "I don't want to talk about it." It's one thing to tell her I'm upset and let her see me crying. It's another thing to tell her a secret, especially since she's proven in the past that she can't keep them to save her life.

"Okay." She nods, seemingly accepting this. She opens the peanut butter cups and offers me one.

I take it.

"Well, do you think it can be fixed?" she asks.

I think about it. I kissed someone else. I *kissed someone else*. Can it be fixed? I guess, technically, it can. I mean, there are couples who get over someone cheating and stay together. But those couples have usually been married for, like, years and years, and they have kids, and they don't want to mess up their families. But still. It's not like I slept with someone else. It was just a kiss. Although, if I'm being honest with myself, I've never bought into that whole "it was just a kiss" excuse. If you ask me, cheating is cheating.

"I don't know," I say.

Aven nods, then nibbles around the outside of her peanut butter cup.

Suddenly, I feel like I want to change the subject.

"Did you tell Liam you're in love with him?" I blurt.

Her face darkens for a moment, but then a little smile plays on her lips. "You remembered. About my email. What I wanted to do."

"Of course I remembered." Her face brightens even more, and I roll my eyes. "Don't get so excited, it's not like it's something I could forget. You've been in love with Liam since forever."

She shakes her head. "No. I haven't told him yet." She takes in a deep breath. "But I'm going to. And honestly, Lyla, you should tell Derrick the truth. You're not going to be able to work out whatever it is unless you tell him." She waits for me to say something, but when I don't, she stands up and gathers the empty peanut butter cup wrappers. "I'm going to go grab breakfast." She squeezes my shoulder. "Good luck," she calls before disappearing down the hall.

"Thanks."

I know she's right.

I have to tell Derrick.

It's just going to be horrible.

I take a few seconds to wipe my eyes and make sure I have my crying under control before heading back into the room. After I close the door behind me, Derrick rolls over and stretches his arms over his head. Blink, blink, blink. I will not cry, I will not cry, I will not cry. I throw myself down on the bed next to him and bury my face in the covers so he can't see my face. La, la, la, not about to cry.

"I missed you," Derrick says, and pulls me close.

I'm an awful person. I'm a horrible person. I should be punished. I have to tell him. Right? Yes. I definitely have to tell him. And I have to do it before Juliana does.

Except . . . maybe I *don't* have to tell him. I mean, it's going to be my word against hers. She has no *proof* that I kissed Beckett. And what would really be the point of telling Derrick and getting him all worked up? I don't even like Beckett. He's cocky and smarmy and every girl he looks at wants him. No one goes through life getting any girl they want and becomes a nice person. It's, like, impossible. You know, formatively.

He even said himself that he doesn't want girls to put any expectations on him. So I just won't ever talk to him again. It's kind of perfect. When you think about it, not tell-ing Derrick is probably the best idea. I'll just . . . deny it. Like, for Derrick's own good. Not mine. It's actually very unself-ish of me.

What if he believes Juliana over you?

He wouldn't. Would he?

I feel my face starting to do that thing again—where my lips gets all wobbly and my eyes crinkle up on the sides. Now that Aven's brought it to my attention, I can tell she's right. It's true—I do have a face I make right before I'm about to cry.

Derrick kisses me softly on the head. "I'm gonna go back to my room to take a shower," he says. "And then maybe we can head out and get some breakfast."

The doughnuts and orange juice I had this morning are lying heavily in my stomach. After all that sugar and kissing and lying, I'm definitely not hungry. But it would be weird to refuse breakfast. It's usually my favorite meal of the day.

"Sounds great," I say. "I'm starving!" My voice sounds squeaky, like a mouse. I sound like a liar. A huge liar.

But if Derrick notices anything, he doesn't show it. He just sits up in bed, then stretches his arms over his head again and yawns. His muscles flex under his shirt. God, he is so good-looking. *Not as good-looking as Beckett.* The thought enters my brain before I can get rid of it, like a fly at a picnic. I squash it, then stand up and give Derrick a kiss on the mouth.

"Have fun!" I say brightly.

He frowns but then smiles. Probably he thinks I'm kissing him because I want to warm him up for our sexcapades later. "I'll text you when I'm done with my shower."

I won't hold my breath.

God, what is going on with my thoughts? I really need to learn how to control them. Maybe I should take one of those meditation classes they're always advertising on the bulletin board at school. Of course, those classes are for people who have anger management problems. We had a bunch of fistfights break out last year, and the administration went crazy and started implementing all these new programs. But if you can learn to control your anger, shouldn't you be able to learn to control your sexual desires? I have a vision of me sitting in the gym at our school on a disgustingly dirty yoga mat (the school provides them and no way are they washed properly), surrounded by guys who want to punch each other.

As soon as Derrick's gone, I decide that I need to get ahold of myself.

Nothing bad has happened yet.

Yes, I kissed another guy. Yes, Juliana saw me. But she hasn't told Derrick. And I need to keep it that way. It's like getting ahead of a story.

I reach over and grab my phone, immediately dialing Juliana.

"*Hola, chica,*" she says when she answers. Her voice has a

tiny little lilt to it, like she knows why I'm calling and she's going to enjoy holding this over my head.

I immediately go on the offensive. "Holy shit!" I say really enthusiastically, because Juliana responds to drama and over-the-top proclamations. "Can you believe Beckett did that?"

"Did what?" she teases, like she doesn't know. I resist the urge to march down to her room and throttle her.

"Kissed me! I mean, holy crap! Like, why did he think that was okay?"

"I have no idea," Juliana says. "Derrick will kill him."

"I know," I agree, glad that she's maybe buying into my version of events, the one starring me as the hapless victim and Beckett as the arrogant womanizer who needs to get his ass kicked. "I haven't told Derrick yet. Do you think I should?"

"Hmmm." She draws out the word nice and slow, like she's really thinking about it. "I don't know."

"Me neither." I pretend I'm thinking about it. "I mean, I want to. But he would just get all upset and probably go after Beckett."

"Mmm," she murmurs. "What were you guys doing on the beach together anyway?"

"We weren't together!" I yell. "I mean, um, I was just out getting some coffee and doughnuts. And then I ran into Beckett."

"Wow. He's, like, stalking you. Maybe you *should* tell Derrick."

"Maybe," I say, my heart sinking.

There's a long silence.

"Actually, maybe you shouldn't," she says. "Like you said, it will just upset him."

"Yeah." I let out my breath in relief.

"Anywaysies, a bunch of us are going to brunch, then we're going to lie on the beach and get tan. You wanna?"

"Um, no thanks," I say. I'd rather poke my eyes out with toothpicks. "I'm supposed to meet Derrick in a few."

"Maybe I'll see you later then," she says. I'm sure it's just my imagination, but her voice sounds ominous.

"Oh, yeah, definitely." Not.

I hang up the phone. I should feel relieved. I mean, it doesn't seem like Juliana's going to tell Derrick what she saw. And yes, that doesn't really solve the problem of whether I should tell him, but at least it gives me options.

But why was she so okay with not telling him? And why didn't she . . . I don't know, threaten me or something? Like tell me that if I don't end up telling him, she will? She's supposed to be Derrick's good friend. In fact, she's much better friends with him than she is with me. So then why isn't she demanding I tell him? Is it possible she's going to tell him anyway?

This whole vacation is getting way too complicated. This

trip is supposed to be fun, not some kind of drama-filled exercise in ex-friends and revenge and cheating. I shake my head. I need to refocus. I came here to connect with my boyfriend, and maybe even possibly lose my virginity. Yes, there have been a few setbacks and detours, but the simple facts remain the same. There are two days left on this trip, and I should be able to finagle all I want to accomplish into the next forty-eight hours. *You can't sleep with Derrick unless you tell him you kissed Beckett. And you need to really think about why Juliana is okay with you not telling him.*

I push those thoughts right out of my mind and head into the bathroom, where I turn the shower as hot as it can go and step under the spray. There's an array of posh-looking shampoos and conditioners sitting on a little shelf that's slung over the shower faucet, and I paw through them. Wow. Kiehl's and everything. You'd think the school would have chosen a hotel that was a little bit cheaper, but I guess they had to make it expensive so people's parents wouldn't freak out thinking about them stuck in some crappy motel room. Not that I'm going to complain. I mean, Kiehl's!

I lather up my hair and then take extra time to condition it really well. Usually I just slap the conditioner in and then rinse it out, but not today. Today I make sure I comb it through every strand with my fingers so that it gets evenly distributed.

Then I rinse it all out and take my time blow-drying

until my hair is almost stick straight. When I'm done blow-drying, I plug in the straightener that either Aven or Quinn left in the bathroom and slide it down my hair, piece by piece. God, why don't I do this more often? My hair looks awesome when I do it this way.

When I'm done, I dress carefully for the day, putting on my bathing suit and then slinging my wrap over it. The wrap is gorgeous—it's cream-colored and flowy and shows just enough to be sexy without being over the top.

Once I'm dressed I take a really long time applying my makeup, even doing this smoky eye tutorial that I found on YouTube, like, a bazillion years ago but never really had the patience to try. When I'm done with my makeup, Derrick still hasn't texted me. So I take the extra time to do some contouring. I've always wanted to try contouring—it's when you use your blush to create shadows on your face so that your cheekbones really pop and make you look crazy skinny.

I don't have any blush, so I use bronzer instead. Wow. I kind of look like a model. I shake my head in disgust at the messages the media send us. Making everyone think that celebrities are so much prettier than us when all you need is a contouring brush, some YouTube videos, and a little time. And voilà!

But people think they can't look just as good. Well. You probably can't every single day. It takes forever to do all this. And now that I'm looking closer, my bronzer does look kind of caked on. But whatever. It's Florida. Everyone here has a tan. And a lot of people here are wearing lots of makeup.

When in Rome, right?

I spritz perfume all over myself, then help myself to the makeup-setting spray that's sitting on the counter. I need it, especially if I'm going to be out in the sun all day.

I give myself a smile in the mirror, then head back out into the room. I'm not sure what exactly to do now, though. Should I text Derrick? I pace around a little bit, trying to keep my thoughts from straying to where they want to go. Which is to Beckett. And our kiss.

You weren't doing all those makeup tutorials because you wanted to look good for Derrick. You were doing them to keep your mind off Beckett. How his lips felt. How his hands pulled you close. How the stubble on his chin was ridiculously sexy, and how he tasted like oranges and sugar and danger.

I start pacing faster. I need to get out of here before my mind explodes.

I decide to go to Derrick's room. Who cares if he's ready? I'm done playing games.

I clomp down the hall and into the elevator (I'm wearing my pink flip-flops, which for some reason have started hurting my feet—maybe I just need to break them in?), then take it down to Derrick's room.

I put on what I hope is my sexiest smile, then grab the door frame and lean against it, pulling the top of my cover-up down so that my cleavage juts out just enough to be tempting.

Then I knock on the door.

Silence, then a bunch of rustling from inside the room.

The door flings open.

"Oh," Beckett says, his lips turning up into that sexy grin of his. "Hello there. Back for more, are you?"

My eyes widen, and I immediately push my boobs back into the top of my bathing suit. Well. As much as I can. There's only so much you can do when your bathing suit is this inappropriate.

"Where's Derrick?" I demand. Crap. I really thought Beckett would still be out on the beach.

But part of you was hoping he'd be here.

Lies, lies, lies! God, my brain is a real mess today. I wonder if I'm coming down with multiple personality disorder. Like, one of my personalities is totally normal and loves Derrick and is excited about this trip. My other personality is some kind of sex-crazed maniac who can't seem to keep her boobs inside her top and wants to kiss and cheat with every guy she sees.

Not every guy. Just Beckett.

Ahhh!

"He's in the bathroom," Beckett says. He's not wearing a shirt. Beckett. Is. Not. Wearing. A. Shirt. His body is ridiculously perfect. His biceps flex against the door, and his chest is smooth and tan and defined. His flat stomach shows the perfect hint of a six-pack before narrowing to a V and disappearing into the navy-blue shorts he's wearing.

My other personality is ridiculously turned on at the sight of it.

"Oh."

"Would you like to come in and wait?"

Yes. "No."

"Should I send him back to your room then?"

"What's taking him so long?"

"I don't know." He shrugs. Then he glances behind him and steps out into the hallway, shutting the door behind him. I take a step back, but he's still crazy close to me. So close I can feel the heat coming off his bare chest through the thin material of my cover-up.

I know I should take another step back, but his eyes are mesmerizing me. They're, like, holding me hostage right where I'm standing. Maybe he has superpowers. Like he's some kind of paranormal romance hero. What? It could happen. I'm sure Bella was totally surprised, too, and it probably didn't really kick in until she was giving birth to her vampire baby. If I have a vampire baby, I hope my other personality is in charge that day.

"Listen," Beckett says, "I'm sorry. For what happened on the beach. It was stupid."

"It was *ridiculously* stupid," I say. I point my chin into

the air haughtily. "I have a boyfriend. So that was very inappropriate."

He nods. "I don't . . . that's not something that I do a lot. You know, try to hook up with girls who have boyfriends." Then he sighs and rubs his hands over his face. "Actually, that's not true. I do try to hook up with girls who have boyfriends a lot. But I shouldn't have done that to you."

He's an ass. I won't forgive him. "That's disgusting," I say. "You shouldn't try to hook up with girls who have boyfriends! Why would you do that?"

He blinks at me and looks surprised, like no one's ever asked him that before. His lashes are long and full. It doesn't seem fair that they would be wasted on a boy. Of course, all they do is serve to make him hotter. His face is so chiseled and manly that the lashes take away the edge. And they seem to fit with his gorgeous green eyes.

"I don't know," he says. "I guess because of that whole thing I said before . . . you know, no expectations."

"Wait a minute." I shake my head in disgust. "You were trying to hook up with me because you thought I wouldn't have any expectations?" Wow. What did he think I was going to do, just go somewhere with him and let him make out with me and then never talk to me again? I mean, wow.

"No!" He looks shocked. "No, that's not why."

"Liar!" This guy is seriously messed up. I wonder if he's some kind of psychopath. Or sociopath. Which is the one that is all charming and good-looking and used to getting their way until they end up chopping you into a little pieces after months of playing with your head?

"I swear," he says. "Lyla, I wouldn't have done that to you."

"Why not?"

"Because I just wouldn't have." His eyes bore into mine, and everything stops except the beating of my heart. "I kissed you because I wanted to. Not because I didn't want there to be expectations. In fact, I kind of want you to have expectations." I can feel the hotel carpet sliding away. Everything is fading into oblivion. It's just me and Beckett, standing here.

And then I come crashing down to earth. "So you kissed me because you wanted to, but now you've decided you shouldn't have done it?" How does that make any sense? My head is starting to hurt.

He opens his mouth to say something, but I cut him off.

"Whatever," I say. "I need to find my boyfriend."

I push by Beckett into the bedroom and over to the bathroom. The door is closed, and I can hear the sound of the shower running. But I can also hear Derrick's voice. Which is weird. Why would Derrick be talking to someone in the shower?

I knock on the door. "Derrick!" I say, hoping my voice doesn't betray any of the chaos that's going on inside me.

"I'm here. I'm ready for breakfast and the beach!" I take a deep breath and try to calm myself. I sound like a crazy person.

"Lyla?" comes the reply. He sounds surprised. The door opens and he peeks out. "What are you doing here?"

"You were taking forever," I say. "So I came to find you." Then I remember I'm supposed to be seducing him tonight, so I quickly resume the pose I had when I first got here. Hand on the door frame, boobs pushed forward, smile on my face. I lick my lips in what I hope is a sexy way. "I'm ready." I don't add *for the beach* this time. *I'm ready* sounds like I'm ready for anything. I'm hoping it will put all sorts of bad thoughts into his head.

"Okay." He holds up his phone. "Just give me a second. I'm on the phone."

"Who are you talking to?" My voice sounds strangled. Juliana! He must be talking to Juliana! The bitch probably called him as soon as she hung up with me. Has she told him yet? He doesn't seem mad. Or upset. And he hasn't beaten up Beckett.

A look of weirdness passes over Derrick's face, and then his forehead wrinkles up. "What's all over your face?"

"What do you mean?" My hands fly to my face. Did I accidentally get chocolate on it or something? I haven't had any chocolate. Oh my god. Maybe it's doughnut dust! There might be doughnut dust on my face! How am I going to explain that? I peek into the bathroom and look at myself in the mirror.

Oh. It's not doughnut dust at all. It's all the contouring I did with my bronzer. Wow. I didn't realize how dark it was. It's a little . . . streaky, too.

"That's just my bronzer," I say defensively.

"What happened to it?" Derrick asks. "It looks a little . . . messy."

"Well, it's hard to get it perfect," I say dismissively. "It will all even out once we're out in the sun."

"Okay," Derrick says, not really looking convinced. He leans in and gives me a kiss. He tastes like toothpaste and smells like soap. "You'll look hot with a tan."

I flush with pleasure. "But, um, who are you talking to?"

"My mom." Yes!! "Just give me a minute and I'll be done."

Derrick looks over my shoulder and I turn, too. Beckett's sitting on the bed, watching our exchange. Derrick glares at him, then kisses me again. "I think maybe you should wait in the hall," he says.

"Good idea."

He closes the bathroom door.

I intentionally don't meet Beckett's gaze. I need to stop this craziness that's been going on. I need to get this vacation back on track, and there's no way I'm going to be able to do that if I have any contact with Beckett.

Snip. I pretend there's some kind of thin string that's

connecting me to Beckett and I've just snipped it. And the thing about a string is that you can't put it back together. Once it's severed, it's severed. There's no going back. It's just . . . done. So that's that.

I'm almost to the door when he comes up behind me.

"I changed my mind," he says into my ear. His breath tickles, making the tiny hairs on the back of my neck stand up and my skin feel like it's on fire. "I'm not sorry I kissed you. In fact, I want to do it again."

He doesn't move, just stays there, waiting for me to make a decision. I can feel his lips just inches away from me. All I would have to do is turn around, just turn around slowly, and we would kiss. His lips would be back on mine, his hands would be back in my hair. My body is screaming for his touch, his kiss, his everything. But I can't do it. No matter how I feel physically, how could I kiss another guy with my boyfriend just a few feet away? That's a whole new level of horribleness.

So even though everything inside me is screaming in protest, I summon all my self-control, then open the door and step into the hall.

TEN

OKAY. I FEEL A LOT BETTER NOW.

My heart is calming down, my body doesn't feel like it's all tense, and my stomach has stopped turning and rolling. In fact, I'm relaxed and tranquil. I'm stretched out on the world's longest and softest beach towel, my toes pointed to the ocean, the sun warming my body and turning me a beautiful bronze color. (Slowly, of course. I slathered myself with SPF 45 when we got here. Nothing hot about skin cancer. Or premature aging.)

Derrick is on the towel next to me, and we're listening to music from his phone. All around us, seagulls chirp and swoop, kids play, and people talk and laugh. A group of college kids are throwing a football around a little bit down the beach, just close enough to look scenic, but not close enough that there's a chance the ball is going to get away from them and bonk me in the head.

"This is nice," I say. Who needs some meditation class? I'm so relaxed. I'm so relaxed that I'm almost falling asleep. I reach over and grab my big floppy hat and place it over my face.

"What?" Derrick asks.

"This is nice," I say.

"It's so nice." He reaches over and slides his finger up my arm. "Your skin feels good," he murmurs.

"Your fingers feel good," I try. It's a lie. His fingers don't feel that good. They feel kind of greasy from his sunblock. Or maybe it's sweat. Ewww. I know some people think sweat is sexy, like when you see sweaty bodies and stuff on TV, but to me, it's just gross.

Stop, I tell myself. *You're being too hard on him.*

I prop myself up on my elbow and drag my hand through the powder-white sand. "What do you want to do tonight?" I ask.

"Well," Derrick says, turning toward me. He's wearing dark sunglasses, and his hair is blowing in the breeze. "I was thinking we could get dinner. I found a really nice place right on the water. Then I was thinking ice cream at Big Olaf, then a nighttime walk on the beach."

"Mmm," I sigh. "Sounds perfect."

"It will be." His fingers return to my arm and slide back up, this time stopping in the crook of my elbow, where he starts moving them back and forth, back and forth.

"I can't wait," I say.

He moves in closer to me. "Then we can go back to our room," he says.

"Mine or yours?"

"Ours." He smiles. "I got us a room at a different hotel. So no one will bother us." His fingers start moving faster on my arm, like he's getting excited thinking about it. Why am I so focused on his fingers moving on my arm? I reach out and grab his hand in mine. Still sweaty. I force my thoughts away from the moisture.

"Wow," I say. "That's so amazing." I wonder how we're going to sneak out of our hotel without anyone noticing. But I guess we don't have to actually spend the night at this new hotel. We can just have sex there and then go back to our rooms. As far as I know they haven't been checking to make sure people are back at night, but maybe they have some way of knowing. Or maybe they're going to start tonight.

Derrick takes my hand and pulls it up to his lips, kissing each one of my fingers softly. Then he leans over and kisses me on the lips.

I've now kissed two boys in one day. I've never done anything like that in my life. In fact, until I met Derrick I could hardly imagine kissing one boy in one day, and now here I am running around kissing two! What is wrong with me? Am I losing my mind?

My phone buzzes in the sand next to me, and I turn over

and grab it. My face feels all hot, and I don't want Derrick to notice anything's wrong.

Oh. It's my mom.

Wanting to know how everything is going.

I text her back, letting her know that everything's fine. I add a big smiley face to the end of my text, then hit send. The reply comes immediately. *Great! Have fun, be careful, see you soon!*

For once I'm grateful my mom isn't the type to ask a ton of questions and get all involved in my life. Usually I'm annoyed by the fact that she doesn't seem to show that much interest. But now I'm glad she's not one of those mothers who's overly invested, the kind of mother who ends up knowing your friends and acting like a BFF and wearing all your clothes. I think of me and my mom going out to buy inappropriate bathing suits with each other and almost laugh out loud.

"What's so funny?" Derrick asks.

"Oh, nothing," I say. "Just thinking about . . . nothing." Something tells me thinking about his girlfriend going bathing-suit shopping with her mom isn't going to get him all worked up.

"Tell me more about tonight," I say.

"Well. We're going to have champagne."

"Mmmm."

"And chocolate."

"Yum."

"And strawberries and rose petals."

"Yay!" See? This is going to be amazing. I imagine a super-nice hotel room, one of those posh ones that seems like it shouldn't even be on the beach because you're just going to mess it up with all the sand you're bound to bring in. Rose petals will line the carpet (or maybe it will have dark bamboo flooring—I saw dark bamboo flooring in a movie once and it seemed very nice), and there will be champagne chilling in a bucket.

Derrick will kiss me soft and slow. He'll tell me he loves me (he's said it before—not a lot, but some guys just aren't that great at expressing their feelings all the time, which is fine with me), and then he'll start undressing me, nice and slow. Our bodies will—

"Oh, and I got us one of those Jacuzzi rooms."

"What?"

"You know, those rooms that have Jacuzzis in them? They call it cuddle and bubble or something?"

"Cuddle and bubble?"

"Yeah, you fill up the Jacuzzi with lots of bubbles and then you cuddle." He looks very pleased with himself. "It's supposed to be very sexy."

"It sounds it," I lie. I'm not sure if that actually does sound very sexy. I mean, it seems like if they call it cuddle and bubble, you're supposed to have sex in the Jacuzzi. Like, they make it known that's what's supposed to happen. The thought of losing my virginity in a hot tub where tons of other couples have done it doesn't sound that sexy. And how are you supposed to use a condom when you're in the water? I'm pretty sure condoms aren't waterproof. They never really mentioned that in health class. Probably our health teacher, Mr. Williams, had never heard of cuddle and bubble. That sounds like something that just got invented. Or maybe they only have cuddle and bubble in Florida.

"It's going to be great," Derrick says. His eyes sparkle. "I'm really excited about it."

His phone vibrates on the towel next to him, ruining the mood. He reaches over, glances at it, then sends the call to voice mail.

"Who was that?" I ask. Juliana! It's got to be Juliana! Didn't she say she was going to be on the beach? I look around for her wildly—she could be lurking anywhere.

"No one." He shrugs. "Just my mom. But I'm with you now. I don't want any distractions."

"Weren't you just on the phone with your mom?" I try not to sound suspicious, but let's face it, it sounds kind of shady. It has to be Juliana. Although . . . if she was calling him, why would he lie about it? Is it because she's in love with him, like Beckett said? Are those two having a secret affair? Is Juliana—

"Hiii!" a voice trills. Juliana appears, seemingly out of

nowhere, and plops down in the sand next to us. I'm annoyed she's crashing but also a little bit relieved to see her. If that was her on the phone, then she wouldn't be here just now, would she? So then who was it on the phone? Was it another girl?

I look at Derrick suspiciously. Damn Beckett for putting this idea in my head.

"What's up?" Derrick asks.

"Nada." Juliana is wearing a very inappropriate bathing suit. Like, even more inappropriate than mine. Her top is white, and you can pretty much see through it. "You guys should come farther down the beach," she says. "We're building a sand castle."

"Isn't that what, like, five-year-olds do?" I ask before I can stop myself. I know it's probably not the best idea to antagonize her when I'm counting on her to keep my secret, but it comes out before I can stop myself. Why is she bothering us?

"More like three-year-olds," she says, giving me a smile. "But you know, when you're on the beach, you should really try to stay busy." She gives me a knowing grin.

I gulp. I literally gulp. Like I'm in a cartoon or something.

"That's true," I say.

"So you guys wanna come?" Her tone sounds . . . vaguely threatening. Almost like if we don't go, she's going to do something. I realize that this is my life now—if I don't tell Derrick, Juliana will always have something to hold over me. Why did she have to be on the beach at the exact moment I was with Beckett? Shouldn't she have been in her room, sleeping it off? I decide to stay quiet and let Derrick turn her down.

But to my surprise, he stands up and starts gathering his stuff. "Sure," he says.

"Sure!" I echo brightly.

Ten minutes later we're settled in farther down the beach, and my mood has completely soured. This part of the beach is way too busy—it's right near the bathrooms and the food and all the vacationers.

Two guys from our class, Maddox Hanson and Bentley Green, are throwing a football around, and it keeps whizzing over my head. It's only a matter of time before they break someone's nose. Maybe mine.

Juliana stands up and starts running in between the two of them, making herself a monkey in the middle without even being asked. She laughs and twirls and jumps at the football, looking like a total asshole. Of course all the guys on the beach love it, because her boobs are bouncing around in her completely inappropriate bathing suit.

I shade my eyes from the sun and glance over at Derrick, who's watching Juliana as she bounces.

"Why don't you take a picture, it'll last longer," I grumble before I can stop myself. It's a totally immature thing to say, not to mention the last time I heard someone say it I was probably, like, seven.

"What?" Derrick asks, looking surprised.

"Nothing."

"No, what did you say?"

"*Nothing.*"

"*Fine.*"

There's a little bit of an edge to his voice that I've never heard before. Usually Derrick is totally cool and relaxed. Although I *was* just being kind of a brat. But still. He shouldn't have been drooling over Juliana. I know it's, like, part of a guy's hormones to do things like that, but you'd think he'd at least try to hide it. Maybe this doesn't have anything to do with Juliana at all. Maybe it has something to do with Beckett.

"Hey," I say. "Are you still mad at me about yesterday? I know we didn't get to really talk about what happened."

His face instantly softens. "No, I'm not mad at you."

"Are you sure? I mean, I know it was probably upsetting to find out Beckett gave me a ride." *And for me to lie to you,* I think but don't say. Why bring more attention to that?

"Whatever." Derrick shrugs. "I understand you had no choice but to come with Beckett. And it was really silly of me to assume that something was going on between you guys."

"Really?" I ask automatically. "Why?" Oops.

"I don't know. Beckett is just so . . ." He puts his hands up in the air, like there are no words to describe Beckett. "He dated Katie Wells, you know that, right?"

"So?"

"So that's the kind of girl he goes for."

"Pretty?"

"Yeah. I mean, no! I mean, yes, Katie's pretty. Ah, not as pretty as you, of course."

I narrow my eyes at him. "You mean I'm not good-looking enough for Beckett."

"No." Derrick shakes his head emphatically. "I just mean that Beckett goes for silly girls. The kind of girls who only have two things on their minds—boys and clothes."

But before I probe him further, a shadow falls over my towel. I squint up into the sunlight. I can make out a dark figure against the backdrop of the sun.

Beckett.

My heart leaps into my throat.

But then the figure talks.

"What the hell were you thinking?" It's a girl's voice. A familiar girl's voice. Definitely not Beckett.

I shift on my towel so that the sun isn't blocking my view anymore. It's Quinn. And she doesn't look happy.

"Oh, hi, Quinn," I say pleasantly.

"Don't 'oh, hi, Quinn' me," she says. "What the hell were you doing this morning?"

"This morning?" Derrick frowns. "What were you doing this morning?"

"Nothing," I say. Oh god, oh god, oh god. Here I was, thinking I was going to get away with kissing another boy, and now Quinn is here to blow the whole thing wide open! This whole time I was worried about Juliana, when I forgot that Quinn saw me with Beckett, too. It serves me right. It's my karma. I'm a horrible person, and this is what happens to horrible people. They get their comeuppance.

Quinn narrows her eyes at me, then says, "Can I talk to you alone?"

Derrick puffs out his chest. "Anything you can say to Lyla, you can say to me."

Well. Not *anything.*

"No," Quinn says, shaking her head emphatically. "I need to talk to her alone."

"Sure," I say, hoping I don't sound too eager. I grab my cover-up before following Quinn across the sand.

When we're a few feet away from Derrick, Quinn stops and turns to me like she's ready to talk. I look over my shoulder nervously. Derrick's lying on his towel, drumming his fingers against his stomach to the beat of his music. We should be far enough away that he can't hear us, but I can't be totally sure.

"Wanna go to the snack bar?" I ask Quinn. "I could use a soda."

"Not really."

I roll my eyes. "We're going." Quinn's always been stubborn. If she got it into her head that she didn't want to do something, she would stick to that decision no matter what. So when I was friends with Quinn, I used to back down whenever we had an argument. I knew there was no winning with her, so I would just let her have her way. Why bang my head against the wall if she was just going to win anyway?

But Quinn and I aren't friends anymore.

And I can't have her spouting off in front of Derrick about Beckett. Not that I want to keep the Beckett thing a secret. In fact, I think I'm going to tell him. Derrick. Tonight. For sure. It's the right thing to do. And I can't live with this whole Juliana thing hanging over my head.

Besides, if I tell Derrick tonight when we're all cozy and romantic, he's not going to care as much. He'll see that he's the one I want to sleep with, not stupid Beckett.

A flash of me and Beckett kissing in a Jacuzzi tub enters my mind.

My back is pushed up against the side of the tub, the steam rising out of the water in clouds. He's kissing me, his hands in my hair, his mouth hot and wanting. He leans in and whispers in my ear, "Lyla, you are so beautiful."

No, no, no, no! Must banish all sex fantasies out of my

mind! Hormonal sex fantasies are not allowed here! Unless they involve Derrick.

I try to picture the same scene, only with Derrick. Somehow it's not as good.

"Hello!" Quinn's saying. She's walked a few feet ahead of me toward the snack bar. "Are you coming or not?"

"Yeah, I'm coming." I put my cover-up on as we walk. It's one thing to be wearing an inappropriate swimsuit on the privacy of my own towel. It's quite another to be walking all around the beach in it.

We walk to the snack bar in silence, Quinn always a few steps ahead of me, pushing sand angrily with her feet.

When it's our turn to order, a good-looking guy wearing a crisp white T-shirt leans down and looks through the order window.

"Hey, ladies," he says.

I give him a smile. "Hey," I say.

"What can I getcha?"

"Just a soda," Quinn says, her voice hard. God, what is her problem? She doesn't have to be rude to the guy. He's just being friendly.

His face crumples a little bit, like he's not used to being talked to so harshly. "Don't mind her," I say to him. "She's kind of . . . uptight."

"No, I'm not!" Quinn says.

"We'll also have a bag of chips and a soft pretzel," I say.

My stomach grumbles. Derrick and I stopped for pancakes before the beach, but I guess pancakes and doughnuts and orange juice aren't exactly the kind of fuel that's going to get you through the whole day. It makes sense. Aren't nutritionists always talking about junk carbs? Hmm. It's probably not going to help that I just ordered up some more.

"So listen," Quinn says while the guy goes to get my food. "I just wanted to tell you to please stop following me."

I hate that she's saying please. Sometimes saying please is polite. Other times it's what people say when they want to say something they know you're not going to like and they want to *pretend* they're being polite. "I wasn't following you. Beckett said you might be in trouble, so I wanted to make sure you were okay. Excuse me for caring about you."

"Oh, right, like you just care about me sooo much," Quinn says. She rolls her icy-blue eyes toward the sky.

"I wouldn't want anything bad to happen to you, if that's what you mean."

"Really? Then why did you let me leave the room like that?"

"Like what?"

"Like I was going out to try and find a random guy to hook up with!"

"I'm not your keeper, Quinn," I say. "I tried to say something, but you—"

"That'll be sixteen dollars," the hottie says, returning to

the window with my stuff. He pushes a fountain soda with no top and a bag of chips and a pretzel across the window.

"Sixteen dollars?" I repeat incredulously. "For a bag of chips and a soda?"

"Well, and the pretzel," he says helpfully, like this makes it any better. He's decidedly less cute now that he's trying to rip me off.

I reach into the tiny pocket of my cover-up and pull out a crumpled ten-dollar bill. It's all the money I brought. I left my debit card back at the room, because I didn't want to end up losing it.

"I guess I'll put the chips back," I say sadly.

The hottie removes them from where they're sitting on the window ledge, then pushes some buttons on the cash register. Good-bye, fried carb goodness. I barely knew you.

"Twelve dollars," he says.

I sigh. "I guess I'll put the pretzel back."

He looks at me, aghast. "You can't put the pretzel back! I've already served it."

"Not really." I look at it, sitting there on the counter, its salty softness taunting me. "It's just sitting there."

"Once I take it out of the warmer, I can't put it back in. Health regulations."

"Fine, then I'll put the soda back."

"But I already poured it!"

"Oh, for the love of god," Quinn says. She drops a

ten-dollar bill on the counter in front of me. "Here. Take it."

"Thank you," I say politely.

The guy at the window shakes his head, like he can't believe how much tomfoolery he has to put up with. I can't believe I ever thought he was cute. Or nice.

He gives me eight dollars change, which I hand to Quinn. She shoves it into her bag without looking at me.

I head for one of the picnic tables in the corner and set my food down. "Would you like a bite of pretzel?" I ask once we're sitting down.

"No."

"So what, exactly, do you want to say to me now?" I ask. "You already told me to leave you alone. So I'm leaving you alone. I won't chase you down at any other random guys' houses." I rip off a piece of pretzel and pop it into my mouth. So. Good. I wish I had some mustard, though. I glance around, but I don't see a condiment station. Probably against health regulations.

"Good," Quinn says.

"Where'd you meet that guy anyway? He was seriously hot."

"At a club."

"Really?" I raise my eyebrows. I know I saw how Quinn was dressed last night, and I know that this morning when I found her at that guy's house it was pretty obvious what they were up to, but still. I was halfway expecting that maybe the guy she hooked up with was someone she knew already—a friend of her sister's from college, or someone she met at camp. Not just some random she met in a club.

"Yeah. Why?"

"I dunno. Just doesn't seem like something you'd do."

"Yeah, well, you don't know me anymore."

"Apparently not." I shrug and take another piece of pretzel. "You don't know me either."

"Yeah, since you were cheating on your boyfriend."

"I was not cheating on him! I told you, Beckett came to my room and told me you were in trouble."

"And since when are you such good friends with Beckett?"

"I'm not."

"Does Derrick know?"

"Obviously not."

She shakes her head, like she can't believe Derrick doesn't know. She has a tiny bit of sunburn on her nose, making her freckles stand out and softening the hard look she's giving me. "Well, whatever. I don't have time to get caught up in your drama."

"*My* drama? You're the one who hooked up with some random guy."

She bites her lip, then opens her mouth to say something smart, but then a shadow crosses over her face. She shuts her mouth and stares down at the ground.

"Sorry," I say, shaking my head. "I shouldn't have said

that. It's really none of my business." It isn't. And besides, judge not lest ye be judged or whatever.

"Did you get the email?" Quinn asks softly.

"The one we sent to ourselves? Yeah." I take another bite out of my pretzel. Why is she bringing up the email? And then I remember what she wrote in her email. *Before gradua-tion, I will . . . do something crazy.*

Was her "something crazy" that guy? The one she slept with? That seems risky and a little reckless.

"Are you going to do what it says?" Quinn asks. "Learn to trust?"

A moment passes between us. The kind of moment where you know if you say the right thing, you could end up healing a lot of old wounds. The kind of moment that's hard to come by, the kind of moment you hope you're going to get in a situation like this. It feels like a tennis ball balancing on the net, not sure which way to drop, and it's up to me to tell it what to do.

"Quinn . . . ," I start. But my throat gets choked up. What am I supposed to say to her? What do you say to someone who was like a sister to you? Who you shared everything with? And how can someone you were so close to just be gone from your life, suddenly, like it's nothing? I grope around in my head for the right words to say, something that could do something, anything, to bridge the huge gap that now exists between us.

"Never mind," she says, standing up. Her face is hard again, like she can't believe how stupid I am, and how stupid she was for thinking I could be anything but dumb. "Just stay out of my life, okay?"

And then she's gone.

ELEVEN

"DO YOU WANT TO GO TO A CLUB?"

This is what Derrick says later that night when he comes to my room to pick me up for our big night out.

"Excuse me?"

"A club." He seems very . . . I don't know. Energetic? Frantic? He's wearing a crisp blue button-up and khaki shorts, and he smells like hair gel and cologne. Yum.

"What kind of club?"

"A dance club. A bunch of people are going."

"I thought we were going to dinner," I say, making sure to keep my tone light just in case he thinks all I care about are the material things. "And then to cuddle—to the Jacuzzi room."

"Oh, we are," he says. "But I was thinking we could go dancing in between." He leans in close to me in the elevator. "Come on. Me, you, dancing . . . it will be hot and sexy." His eyes are bright with excitement.

"You don't dance," I tease.

"I'll dance with you."

"*I* don't dance."

"You'll start."

I think about it. Me, Derrick, in some sexy club with house music pumping and strobe lights flashing. We'll order drinks and sip them in the corner, people-watching and talking with our heads close together until we're buzzed enough to head onto the dance floor. Our bodies will become a blur, until we're all hot and bothered and ready to go back to the hotel room, where we'll fall into the Jacuzzi to wash off.

Actually, that sounds disgusting. Why would we wash off in a Jacuzzi? Then we'd just be sitting around in our own filth. Not to mention how many other people have probably used that Jacuzzi to wash off. We'll be sitting in their filth, too. They probably don't even wash the tubs. They probably have a bunch of college kids working there who don't care about things like antibacterial spray. They probably just wipe it with a little water and call it a day.

"So you want to?" Derrick asks. "Go dancing?"

"Sure." Sounds sexy. Sounds fun. I decided to just go with it. Plus, I'm wearing the perfect dancing outfit—a black tank top and a short flippy black skirt. Strappy black sandals that I bought at a little flea market on the street earlier complete the look. I'm a little tan from the beach, and my bronzer has finally started to blend in. I curled my hair into beachy waves, then sprayed the whole thing with tons of hair spray to make sure it would stay. I look Florida sexy and ready for anything.

Derrick takes my hand as we walk out of the hotel and onto the cobblestone walk that leads to the sidewalk. I flush with pleasure at being with him. I remember when Derrick and I first got together sophomore year. It was at a school basketball game, and I was trying to climb up the bleachers with my hands full of food. I tripped and almost landed in his lap, spilling a little bit of soda on him in the process. He didn't care, though. He helped me get my footing, held my soda for me, and then held my hand and walked me to my seat.

Throughout the game he kept coming up the bleachers to check on me, asking me if my legs were okay, joking around that I needed to tell him if I was going to attempt to walk again so he could help me. It was the perfect meet-cute. But my life wasn't a movie, and so I figured I'd probably never talk to him again. We didn't have any classes together, we had no mutual friends, and so there was really no reason for me to run into him. But when I passed him between second and third period the next day, he pulled me over to the side of the hallway.

"Hi," he said.

"Hi." He was holding a copy of *The Grapes of Wrath* in one hand, and the top corner of the book was fraying. I couldn't stop looking at that fraying corner. I felt like I was in a dream—things like this (cute boys coming over to me in the middle of the hallway after I'd spent the whole night thinking about them) never happened to me. But if I were in a dream, there was no way I'd notice something as detailed as a fraying corner of a book. As long as that fraying corner was there, everything that was happening was real.

"Listen," Derrick said, "I'm not going to beat around the bush and be all coy. I haven't been able to stop thinking about you since last night. Do you want to hang out later?"

And that was it.

We have been together ever since.

Everything was perfect.

We were perfect.

Until now.

You cheated on him.

I have to tell him. I know I do. I can't have sex with him while keeping this kind of secret. It's just not right.

By the time we get to the restaurant, a cute little seafood place called the Anchor that's right on the ocean, my stomach is in knots.

"You okay?" Derrick asks once we've been seated.

"I'm fine. I think my feet just hurt a little from walking in these shoes."

"Oh no," he says. "I hope you're still going to be able to dance." He reaches for the menu that's been placed in front of him and slides his eyes down the list. "I want you to get whatever you want. Tonight's special, and so we should celebrate."

I squeeze his hand and give him a big smile. Maybe I shouldn't tell him. I mean, why would I want to ruin such a special night? And honestly, would he really even *want* to know? I remember getting into this huge fight with Quinn once about how if someone cheated on her, she wouldn't want to know about it. We were at a party, playing one of those games where everyone passes around a deck of cards with questions on them, and the whole group has to answer. One of the questions was "If your boyfriend or girlfriend cheated on you, would you want to know?" and Quinn kept insisting she wouldn't, because if the cheating happened it was in the past, and she wouldn't be able to change it, so why would she want to ruin her whole relationship?

I wonder if Derrick would agree.

The waiter appears at our table. He's one of those fancy waiters, the kind that get all mad if you order your steak well done because they think you're ruining the meat. How can you be ruining the meat if that's the way you like it? I like my meat well done. I can't help it.

"What would you like to drink?" the waiter asks. He has two gray hairs growing out of his nose.

"Ummm . . ." I let my eyes wander over to the wine list, but he gives me a disapproving look. Whatever. I didn't want alcohol anyway. I need to keep my wits about me. "Just a Shirley Temple."

"Coke," Derrick says.

"Very well," the waiter says, like he can't believe what idiots we are.

"So," Derrick says once the waiter is gone. He reaches across the table and takes my hand. "I'm really glad I'm here with you."

"I'm really glad I'm here with you, too."

His fingers massage the inside of my wrist gently. Mmm. That feels good. I feel the tension in my shoulders and back instantly start to dissipate. See? This is going to be fine. This is going to be great. Derrick reaches out and fingers the beads of my tigereye bracelet and I pull back like I'm on fire.

"What's wrong?" Derrick asks.

But the waiter reappears with our drinks before I can answer.

"Are you ready to order?" he asks. He doesn't look like he's ready to *take* our order. He doesn't have a pad out or anything. I hate when waiters don't write down your order. They always end up messing it up, and then you have to be a jerk and send your food back when they're the ones who should have just written it down in the first place.

I haven't even looked at the menu, but Derrick surprises me by saying, "Yes, we're ready. We're both going to have the filet mignon, one cooked well done, one cooked medium rare. And we'll have the garlic mashed potatoes and corn for the table."

"Excellent, sir," the waiter says, sounding like he thinks it's anything but.

"So what do you think?" Derrick asks once he's gone. "This is a nice place, right?"

What do I think? I think I wanted to order my own damn food is what I think. What is this, the 1950s? Who orders garlic anything on a night when they're going to be having sex for the first time? Garlic definitely doesn't scream sexy. And they had some really good-looking truffle mac and cheese that I was dying to try. What happened to me being able to get whatever I want?

"This place is great," I lie.

"I hope you don't mind that I ordered for you. I heard the filet mignon is amazing." He picks up my hand and kisses my fingers softly. "I thought it would be romantic."

"It was." I guess.

My body starts to feel filled with a weird energy, and my leg is jittering up and down under the table. It knocks against the bottom, and our water glasses vibrate.

"You okay?" Derrick asks. "You seem nervous. Are you nervous?"

"About tonight? No." It's true. Who has time to be nervous about losing my virginity? That's the last thing I'm nervous about. The first thing I'm nervous about is the fact that I'm about to lose my virginity to a boy I've been cheating on. Well, *cheated* on. "Been cheating on" seems like it's ongoing. Which it most certainly is not.

"Are you sure? Because we can talk about anything, Lyla. You know that, right?"

His eyes look so sincere, like he really does mean I can tell him anything. *Tell him. Do it. Do it now.* Okay. I'm going to. Right now. Now. Right this second.

"Do you want to play a game?" I blurt.

Derrick looks confused, and then realization dawns on his face. "You mean like a sex game?" He shakes his head. "I don't know. I mean, it sounds fun, but I'm not sure we should do anything that might get us hurt. Especially the first time." He cocks his head, considering. "But maybe we could do it on the second try. You know, later tonight."

"No." I shake my head. "I mean, like a game of *questions*." I'm so brilliant. All I have to do is pretend that I'm asking a hypothetical question about whether Derrick would want to know if he was being cheated on. Like I did with Quinn at that party. And then when I find out his answer, I'll know what to do.

"You mean like truth or dare?"

"Sort of." Sigh. This is going to be harder than I thought. Too bad I don't have that game with me—it would be a lot easier to explain. And then I have my second brilliant idea in the span of just a couple of minutes.

"It's this new app," I lie. I pull my phone out of my purse and pretend I'm pulling up some imaginary app. But I accidentally start one of my playlists, and "All the Single Ladies" by Beyoncé comes blaring out of the speaker. The middle-aged couple next to us looks over and gives us a dirty look. "Sorry," I say.

"You seem frazzled," Derrick says. He reaches over and takes my hand. "If you're not ready . . ."

"No, no, I'm ready!" I say. We need to focus here. "I just thought it would be fun to play a game. You know, to, uh, relax me." I clear my throat. "Okay, it's one of those games where you ask the other person questions."

"Like 'Have You Ever?'" Derrick asks. "Isn't that a drinking game?"

"Kind of like that," I say. "But they're more, uh, in-depth questions. Okay, so for example . . ." I look at my phone, like I'm about to read a questions off my imaginary app. Actually, if there's no app like that, there should be. Maybe I should create it. Then I could play the game anytime I wanted. Or better yet, maybe I'll create a fake one. For situations just like this. It would probably make me tons of money. What should I ask Derrick, though? I can't just lead off with the cheating question. That would be too obvious.

"Um, if you caught one of your friends stealing at work, would you tell on them?" I try.

"Of course," he says. "Stealing is wrong."

"Yeah, but what if it was your *friend*?"

"My friend stealing is still wrong." He takes a sip of his Coke.

"What if it was me stealing? Would you turn me in?" The thought of Derrick betraying me is almost comforting. Like his hypothetically getting me fired cancels out the actual, real-life kissing that I did.

"I might try to talk to you first," Derrick says, "and tell you to stop. But if you kept stealing, I would have to do the right thing. You should always do the right thing."

Oh god, oh god, oh god.

"Don't you agree?"

"Oh, yeah, definitely. I would totally turn someone in who was stealing." It's a lie. Why would I turn in a friend who was stealing? Actually, why would I be friends with someone like that in the first place? I get annoyed that the game includes a question that makes no logical sense, and then I remember it's a fake app and that I made it up.

"Okay, next question!" I sound a little crazed. "Okay, next question," I say quietly. "If someone was cheating on you, would you want to know about it?"

He frowns. "If someone was cheating on me?"

"Yeah, like if your girlfriend, uh, was . . . if hypothetically she cheated on you."

"Why?" Derrick grins. "Are you cheating on me?"

"No!" Great. Now not only have I lied by omission, I've

actually lied straight out. Although the way he phrased it made it seem like he was asking if I was cheating, present tense. Which I'm not. So maybe I can get off on a technicality. Is it hot in here? It feels very hot in here.

"I know you would never cheat on me," Derrick says tenderly. "That's why I'm so sorry for acting the way I did yesterday. You know I trust you, right?"

"Of course." Pause. He's not answering the question, though. He needs to answer the question. "So what's the answer?"

"What answer?"

"The answer to the question. About cheating."

"But I just said you would never cheat on me."

Why does he have to be so literal? "Yeah, but it's not . . . you're not supposed to think of it that way. It's supposed to be a hypothetical girlfriend."

"But I don't have a hypothetical girlfriend. I have you."

"Well, the girlfriend you're going to have after me."

He blanches. "Why would I have a girlfriend after you?" His eyes meet mine across the table, the light from the flickering cream-colored votive candles illuminating the sincerity on his face. Does he mean he might marry me? He wants to marry me! He would be such a good husband. And a dad, too. I'll bet he'd be super involved in our kids' lives.

And I would look so good in a mermaid-style wedding dress. I've always wanted one of those. With a separate dress for the reception, of course. No one can dance in a mermaid-style wedding dress. Not that I know how to dance. Good thing we're going to a club. Maybe I can pick up some moves.

The waiter comes over with our food.

Wow.

That was really fast.

I take a bite of mashed potatoes. Delicious.

"Good?" Derrick asks, smiling.

"Perfect."

I don't think I should tell him. I mean, it's one thing to cheat on your high school boyfriend. It's quite another to cheat on your future husband.

We stay at dinner for another hour, ordering dessert and laughing and reminiscing. Things have completely and totally relaxed between us. There's no tension in my body, and there's no tension between us from yesterday.

We're just . . . happy.

As we walk to the club, I inhale the warm night air and the scent of the ocean. I don't know what I was thinking, letting Beckett kiss me like that. Did I even let him? It's starting to feel very foggy now. The bouncer in front of the club doesn't ID us, which I think is cool until I realize it's not a twenty-one-and-over club. Everyone who's twenty-one gets a green wristband on their wrist so the bartender knows they can drink. But the bouncer doesn't even ask if we want one. I must look young.

No matter.

I don't need booze tonight.

I'm drunk on love.

The inside of the club is exactly how I pictured it. Red leather couches line the perimeter, and there are floating tables hooked to the walls in between in each one. Matching leather ottomans are scattered around the room at random intervals, giving the club a casual but sophisticated feel. It's actually not that crowded, but that's probably because it's still early. Nothing really gets going around here until eleven, and it's only ten.

"Let's sit over there," Derrick says, pointing to a booth in the corner. As soon as we sit down, he leans into me. "I missed you yesterday," he breathes. "I can't wait to be with you later."

"I can't wait either," I say.

When the cocktail waitress comes around, Derrick orders me another Shirley Temple and himself another Coke.

"You wanna dance?" he asks.

"Maybe in a few minutes," I say, not quite ready to get out there yet. I watch as a girl wearing a lime-green belly shirt grinds against a girl in black leather shorts. The Kesha remix that's pounding through the club seems like it was made for them. Hopefully the really good dancers get here early, and then by the time everyone else shows up, everyone will be on equal footing. Plus, as people start getting drunker I'm sure their dance skills are going to start deteriorating. That will be my excuse if I'm a really bad dancer. I'll just pretend I've been drinking.

After a while, the club starts to get busier and a little hotter, so I pull off the black shrug I'm wearing.

"Yum," Derrick says, kissing my bare shoulder.

"Mmm," I breathe, trying to ignore the fact that he said the word "yum." Yum is not sexy. Yum is what you say when you eat an ice cream. I am not an ice cream.

Derrick's hand is on my bare leg, and it's inching up ever so slowly, moving higher and higher until finally it's pushing up the bottom of my skirt. I sigh and force myself to relax until my body starts to respond to his touch. I'm falling into that kind of woozy state where I can feel the music pulsing through me and I'm hot and sleepy and semi-turned on and sort of zoning out.

And that's when Beckett walks into the club, ruining everything.

TWELVE

HE'S WEARING BAGGY JEANS AND A BLACK T-shirt and black shoes that look like the kind of thing you should be wearing to a business meeting. They're shiny and new, and they contrast with the casualness of his outfit, even though his T-shirt looks totally expensive. He oozes confidence, and he stands there surveying the room like he's waiting for people to notice him. Actually, that's not true. People just *are* noticing him. A couple of girls who are sitting next to us sit up and whisper to each other. Probably about how hot he is.

My skin starts to feel itchy and hot. Why is he here? Why did he have to come to *this* club on *this* night? Why is Siesta Key so damn small? Why couldn't we have had our senior trip at Disney World or something? That place is huge and has, like, five million different parks. I could definitely have avoided him there.

I pull back from Derrick so I can ask him if he wants to get out of here and go back to the hotel. I'm ready to leave. Yes, we haven't danced yet, but who cares? Dancing is overrated, anyway.

But before I can say anything, Derrick says, "I didn't know Beckett and Katie were back together."

It's so unexpected that I don't register it at first. Then I look back over toward the door.

And there they are.

Beckett.

And Katie Wells.

Together.

She's wearing one of those flapper dresses, the kind that has a top that fits your body like a tight sleeve, then flares out and ends in fringe at the bottom. She has the exact type of body that kind of dress looks good on—tall and slender and willowy. Her dress is white, and every time the strobe lights pass over her, they illuminate the dress, broadcasting to the world just how pretty she is.

"I don't think they're together," I say.

"They're holding hands," Derrick points out.

I look. They are. They're holding hands.

Seething rage fills my body. How dare he hold her hand after kissing me this morning? I pay no mind to the fact that I have a boyfriend, or that I'm planning on having sex with him tonight. Beckett *kissed me* this morning. He shouldn't be here with Katie, or anyone. What a jackass.

I feel like I'm going to cry, which makes no sense. I have no right to be upset. I know that, which almost makes it worse. I'm not only upset and sad, but I'm mad at myself for being upset and sad.

I need to get out of here.

I turn back to Derrick to tell him I want to leave at the same time he says to me, "You wanna dance?"

And then I realize I can't leave. If I ask to leave now, it's going to make it seem like I want to leave because Beckett's here. And if I make it seem like I want to leave because Beckett's here, it's going to be obvious that Beckett has some kind of effect on me.

"I don't know," I hedge. "'I'm getting tired."

"Oh, come on," he says. "I'll lead." What is wrong with him? Shouldn't he be hustling me out of here so that he can take me back to our hotel room and have his way with me? Actually, now that I think about it, he's been stalling all night. Why? Is there something wrong with me? Did Derrick change his mind? Does he not want to have sex with me after all?

"You don't know how to lead," I say crankily.

"Sure I do."

"How?"

"Let me show you."

I hesitate. "Okay," I say finally, even though dancing is

the last thing I want to do. I'm in a horrible mood. Hasn't Beckett ruined enough of my vacation? Making me ride on a motorcycle with him? I could have been killed. Kissing me and almost ruining my relationship? Causing me to get into a fight with Quinn? I mean, isn't enough enough?

Derrick takes my hand and pulls me onto the dance floor. As soon as we get out there, the DJ turns the strobe lights to a slow, lazy rhythm, and a song starts playing that I've never heard before. It has a slow, melodic beat. Derrick wraps his hands around my waist and I rest my head against his shoulder. Since it's such a slow song, I don't really have to do much. I just lean into Derrick's body and sway when he sways. I guess it might be true that he knows how to lead. Well. If leading means just dragging me across the dance floor, which honestly is fine with me.

Derrick turns me around, and I lock eyes with Beckett.

He's sitting near the wall, his legs hanging over the side of the leather couch, his shoulders kind of slouched, like he's not sure yet if he's committed to staying here.

His eyes burn into mine, and a searing want floods my body.

I close my eyes tight. I don't want to see Beckett. Not now.

I pull back from Derrick. "Are you ready to go?" I whisper.

"What?" he asks. He's leaning in so close to me that I can smell the Coke on his breath.

"Are you ready to go?"

"Just a couple more songs," he says. "I don't want to rush this night."

What is he talking about? What guy doesn't want to rush the night he's going to have sex? Aren't guys always trying to rush things? Especially now that it's just hours away. Doesn't he realize that he could take me back to his room right now and have his way with me?

We dance a few more songs. During the fast ones I do my best to bop along to the music. There are so many people on the dance floor now that they're blocking my view of where Beckett is sitting. And after a little bit, I forget he's even there. Well. Sort of. At least enough so that I can calm down a little.

"Are you ready now?" I ask Derrick about twenty minutes later. "I really want to go, I think."

"You sure?"

"Yeah."

This time, Derrick doesn't try to fight it. He nods.

"I'm going to run to the bathroom," I say.

"Okay," Derrick says. "I'll go and pay the tab and grab your sweater."

"Thanks." I squeeze his hand and then head to the ladies' room.

Of course there's a line.

I stand in it, gathering my hair up into a sweaty ponytail

and pushing it up off my neck. The air is cooler back here, and it feels good.

When I finally get into the bathroom, Katie Wells is there, standing in front of the mirror, reapplying her lipstick. Her cheeks look dewy and glowing, the kind of glow you see on Jennifer Lopez or Beyoncé. It's either natural or she has tons of money to spend on cosmetics. And flapper dresses.

I ignore her and head into one of the stalls. I take my time even though there's a line, hoping that by the time I come out, she'll be gone.

But she's not. She's still standing in front of the long mirror that's mounted over the sinks, her makeup spread out on the shelf that's jutting out from the wall. It's like she thinks the space is just for her. Whatever.

I take a deep breath and head to the sink to wash my hands.

When I'm done, I look around, but Katie's blocking the only paper towel dispenser. There are some hand dryers on the other side of the bathroom, but they're both being used.

I think about just leaving the bathroom, but then where am I going to dry my hands? On my dress? No, thank you.

The same rage I felt when Beckett walked into the club bubbles up inside me. Who does she think she is, taking up the whole bathroom like that? And in front of the towel dispenser on top of it? What if someone came in and they had to clean up their baby and they needed towels to do it?

Not that someone would bring a baby to a club, but still. It just really speaks to the way she has no regard for how people are feeling. She's so selfish. She's always been selfish. I vaguely remember sophomore year her asking if she could have extra time on her English assignment because her family was going on a cruise. Can you imagine? Like she couldn't work on the boat? It wasn't even that big of an assignment.

She's probably used to getting things handed to her because she's blond and has dewy cheeks. Well. Not any-more.

"Excuse me," I say to her, all sickly sweet. "I need to get a paper towel for my hands."

She's leaning over the sink toward the mirror, applying eyeliner to her lower lid. She meets my gaze in the mirror and then moves, like, two inches over to the side, giving me just enough room to get my paper towel.

I take my time drying my hands, then throw the towel away and start to head out of the bathroom. I'm actually kind of disappointed. Adrenaline was coursing through my body—I was ready for her to start something with me. Which is ridiculous. Why would Katie even know anything about me?

And then she calls my name. "Lyla."

I turn. She's not looking at me. She's still lining her eyes.

She's putting way too much of that stuff on. If it's not water-proof, she's going to be in a lot of trouble if it rains. God, I hope it rains. She'd probably look adorable, though, and five different guys would run to get her an umbrella.

"I don't want things to be weird," she says. "But I want to let you know that if you kiss Beckett again, I'm going to be really upset."

I'm not sure if it's my imagination, but suddenly the bathroom seems quieter and emptier.

"I didn't kiss Beckett," I say.

"You did," she says. "On the beach. He told me."

I'm so shocked that for a moment, I can't speak. "No, I didn't. He kissed me."

"Not according to him."

"Well, he's lying."

"Beckett doesn't lie," she says. "He doesn't need to. That's not his style."

"Well, I don't care if it's his *style* or not—he's lying. He kissed me."

"Lyla, give it up. He's not interested in you. You have Derrick. I have Beckett. That's how it's supposed to be." She says the last part with such finality that it's hard not to believe her. It makes sense. Beckett is cool and gorgeous, and she's cool and gorgeous.

My head is spinning and my chest feels tight.

I turn around and run out of the bathroom.

And that's when the tears come.

I must be completely out of it, because when I leave the bathroom, I end up going the wrong way down the hall. When I get to the end of it, there's a side door marked EXIT, so I push it open, and suddenly I'm on a side street between the club and the building next to it.

I take deep breaths and try to stop crying.

What is wrong with me? Why am I getting so upset about a guy I hardly know? Why am I getting so worked up over some jerk who isn't even a thing? Am I really that insecure? I know I'm not. Am I?

My phone starts vibrating.

Derrick. I can't go back into the club. I can't risk seeing Beckett or Katie again. Derrick is going to have to come back here and meet me. He'll wrap me in his arms and take me back to our hotel room. Maybe we'll order in room service strawberries and he'll feed them to me before we get into the Jacuzzi.

But it's not Derrick on my phone.

It's an email alert.

Before graduation, I will . . . *learn to trust*.

Why is that email coming *now*? It was scheduled to come

all day *yesterday*, not today. Before I can stop myself, all the anger and frustration of the last forty-eight hours takes over my body, and I throw my phone onto the ground as hard as I can. The screen shatters into a million pieces.

"Oh!" I exclaim, staring at the shards of glass littering the pavement. "Oh no!" I bend down and turn over my ruined phone. A tiny part of the screen has shattered, and the rest has turned into a web of broken glass. I start to sob, big wracking sobs that threaten to take over my body.

After a moment, I feel a hand on my back. I turn around, expecting to see Derrick. But it's not Derrick. It's Beckett. I want to yell at him for bringing Katie here, for telling her that I kissed him. But suddenly, I don't have the energy.

"I broke my phone," I say dumbly.

"I know," he says. "I saw you smash it." He leans down next to me and surveys the damage. "Definitely wrecked."

I look down at my phone, and my eyes fill with a fresh batch of tears.

"Hey, hey, hey," Beckett says. "No use crying over a broken phone."

"It was the only phone I had," I say. "It had all my pictures on it."

"You'll still be able to save them. Just because the screen is wrecked doesn't mean you can't still plug it in and download everything to your computer."

"Maybe," I say, even though I don't believe it. I can't stop staring at my phone. It's somehow symbolic of this trip. It started off so shiny and exciting, and now it's just lying on the pavement, smashed into a million pieces. Anger bubbles up inside me again, the same anger that made me throw my phone onto the ground. I get a tiny burst of energy. "Leave me alone," I say, and try to stand up. I stumble, but make it to my feet.

"You're bleeding," Beckett says.

I look down. There are two small cuts on my pinkie toe, and a deeper one on my ankle. "I don't care." I start to walk away. I need to get away from him. Every time I'm close to him something bad happens. And I'm done with it. I need him to leave me alone. I need to stay far, far away from him. He's an asshole, and I don't even want to give him the satisfaction of seeing me upset.

"You should get those cuts cleaned out," Beckett says. He grabs the crook of my elbow. "You need help walking."

"No, I don't. It's okay, really. They don't hurt or anything." But my resolve is fading. My cuts are actually throbbing now, and my face is starting to feel all tingly and warm, like I might pass out.

"You should still get them cleaned out." He leads me over to the sidewalk and sits me down on the curb. "I'll be right back," he says. "Are you okay here for minute?"

I nod and look at the cuts on my leg. The ones on my toe aren't that deep, but the one on my ankle is dripping blood.

A couple goes strolling by, holding hands. They look at my bleeding ankle.

"Are you okay?" the man asks. "Do you need help?"

"No, I'm okay," I say. "My friend just went to get me some water."

"Okay." They glance over their shoulders once they're past me, like they're not quite sure they should be leaving. Honestly, *I'm* not quite sure they should be leaving. I'm not doing so good on my own. I mean, I smashed my phone.

I smashed my phone! Oh my god. I am so not a violent person. Smashing your phone is what you do when you have anger problems, like the girls at school who get super upset at teachers when they get sent to the office and push their books and papers onto the floor on their way out. Or the boys who get into fistfights, the ones who caused them to implement that meditation class.

Beckett reappears, holding two bottles of expensive-looking water, a stack of napkins, and three Band-Aids.

"This was the only water they had," he said. "But I'm sure it's better to use bottled, anyway. You don't want your leg getting infected." He uncaps one of the bottles and hands it to me. "Drink," he commands.

"I'm not thirsty." I push my chin up into the air angrily. It's one thing to give in to him making me walk, it's quite another for him to make me drink something.

"I don't care. Drink."

I take a sip of the water. It's the best water I've ever had—cool, crisp, and delicious. I'm not sure if it's because it's expensive, or if it's because I've been in the sweaty club for so long. I don't think the Shirley Temples I was drinking were doing that much to hydrate me.

Beckett pours water onto one of the napkins, then uses it to clean the blood off my leg. "Does it sting?"

I shake my head.

He finishes cleaning my wounds, then expertly applies the Band-Aids. "There," he says. "All better. You should probably get some Neosporin when you get back to the hotel, though."

"I once read that your phone has more disease-causing bacteria on it than a toilet seat," I say. As soon as the words are out of my mouth, I realize how ridiculously stupid they are, and I'm totally mortified. Who *says* something like that?

But Beckett just grins. "Even more reason to get some Neosporin."

I nod.

"So where's Derrick?" he asks.

Jesus. Derrick. I forgot all about him. Definitely not a good sign that I've forgotten about my boyfriend. "He's inside," I say. "He's waiting for me. He's probably going to come out here any second." I can't call him because I smashed my phone. I could ask to borrow Beckett's. But that would be weird—me using Beckett's phone to call my boyfriend.

I expect Becket to leave then, but instead he moves a little closer to me on the curb. "Lyla—" he starts.

"No," I say, shaking my head emphatically, and look down at the street. There's a tiny seashell laying against the curb, and I pick it up and move it back and forth between my fingers. "Please don't."

"Please don't what?"

"Say whatever it is you're about to say."

"How do you know what I'm about to say?"

"Because I've watched a lot of movies."

He frowns. "I don't get it."

"I've watched a lot of movies where the hot guy is about to let the girl down gently, when really he's just being a complete asshole. So I know what you're going to say. And I really don't want to hear it." It feels scary letting my guard down, just putting it all out there like that. But I don't care. It's the truth—I *don't* want to hear what Beckett has to say. Until now, I didn't want him to know the effect he was having on me. But the sting of the rejection speech he's about to give is going to hurt more than letting him know I care.

The side of his mouth twitches into a grin. "You think I'm hot?"

"No!" Yes. "That's not . . . the point is I know you're about to give me some big explanation about why you kissed me and then showed up here with Katie." I'm struggling to keep my voice calm. Because the truth is, I *do* want to hear what he has to say. Even though I know that whatever comes out of his mouth is certain to be full of lies and half-truths and things I can't trust, and even though just a second ago I was so mad I could hardly take it, right now I want to hear what he has to say. I want to keep him here with me as long as possible. Once he gives me his bullshit explanation, he's going to leave. And I'm probably never going to talk to him again.

"Are you going to give me some big explanation as to why you kissed me and showed up here with Derrick?" he asks.

"No."

"Why not?"

"Because Derrick's my boyfriend."

"Semantics."

"And besides, I didn't kiss you—you kissed me."

"You kissed me back."

"No, I didn't."

"Lyla." He says my name as a statement, not a question, and there's not even any annoyance behind it. It's like he's just saying, *Come on, we were both there, let's not play games.* Which is confusing. If he doesn't want to play games, then why does he act like such a game player?

"I have a boyfriend," I say. "I shouldn't have been on the beach with you this morning in the first place. And you shouldn't have told Katie we kissed."

"I told Katie we kissed because I wanted her to know that I'm not interested in her like that." He reaches out and fingers one of the beads on my tigereye bracelet, the same way he did back at the hotel. His touch feels familiar and exciting all at once. My arms break out in goose bumps. "Did you mean what you said about how you shouldn't have been on the beach with me this morning?"

"Yes," I say. But my voice sounds tinny and weird and far away, almost like I'm in an echoey hallway or a movie with bad sound.

"Say it again."

"What?"

"Look at me and tell me you want nothing to do with me."

"That's ridiculous." I look away and down the alley toward the beach. If you look very closely, you can see a slip of ocean in between the buildings, can hear the sound of the waves crashing up against the shore.

"If it's so ridiculous, then do it." I feel him shift slightly forward on the curb, so that his elbows are on his knees. I know that if I look at him, his face is going to be right there, and I'm going to be reminded of kissing him and how amazing it felt. *I'm here with Derrick*, I tell myself. I wonder if I should get a rubber band to keep around my wrist. Then every time I saw Beckett I could snap it. Eventually, I would start to equate the pain with Beckett's face, and I would start avoiding him. It's called aversion therapy. We learned all about it in psychology.

"Why did you come here with Katie?" I blurt.

"Why did you come here with Derrick?"

"Derrick is my boyfriend."

"So? You still showed up here with him, even after you kissed me this morning."

I don't say anything.

"You really see things in black and white, don't you, Lyla?"

"What?"

"You think that because you have a boyfriend, it means kissing me was wrong. You think because I came here with Katie after kissing you, I must be a total jerk. You never stop to think about the whys, do you?"

I shake my head. "I have no idea what you're talking about."

Before graduation, I will . . . learn to trust. That stupid email pops into my head again. I feel like balling my fists up against my head and screaming. I smashed my phone. That email should be gone forever.

"What I'm talking about is that—"

And that's the moment Derrick picks to walk outside and find me sitting there with Beckett.

"Lyla," Derrick says when he sees me. "Are you okay? Where were you? I was getting worried." Then he notices

Beckett sitting next to me. "What is he doing here?"

"He was just leaving," I say.

But Beckett doesn't move.

"Oookaay," Derrick says. "But what is he doing out here?"

"I'm right here, dude," Beckett says, rolling his eyes. "You don't have to talk through me."

Derrick's shoulders stiffen and his back gets straight. Uh-oh. "Fine," he says. "What the fuck are you doing with my girlfriend?"

"Your girlfriend was out here all alone, and she cut her foot. So I was helping her," Beckett says. He stands up. "And if you really gave a shit about her, you would have been out here, too."

"I didn't know where she was!" Derrick says. Then he turns to me. "What are you *doing* out here?"

Good question. What excuse could I possibly have for being out here in a back alley after telling him I was going to the bathroom? Telling him I ran out here because I saw Katie in the bathroom definitely isn't going to go over well. "I got confused," I say. "I opened the wrong door and then I dropped my phone."

I point to where the remnants of my phone are still littering the sidewalk, sparkling under the moonlight that is now shining down into the alley. "And I cut myself," I add.

"Are you okay?" Derrick rushes over and looks at my ankle.

"I'm fine." I don't like the three of us being out here together. It's giving me all kinds of anxiety. Beckett is a complete loose cannon, and who knows if he's going to say something about what really happened. "I just don't really want to be here anymore," I say. "I want to go home."

I mean back to the hotel, or I guess the hotel Derrick got us. But now that I think about it, home *home* wouldn't be that bad either. My room at home is nice—I have thousand-thread-count sheets that I bought with my own money, and a comfy bedspread and a soft chenille throw. I have a TV mounted on my wall and candles on my nightstand and my own bathroom with a huge (albeit outdated) tub. Suddenly I'm so homesick I almost can't stand it.

"Can we please leave?" I ask Derrick. "Please?"

"Lyla—" Beckett starts.

"Beckett, please," I say, shaking my head. "Please, just . . . just go."

He stands there for a second, watching me.

"Please," I say, looking him in the eye. "I mean it, just go."

Something passes over his face, and then he nods slowly before turning and walking away.

"I'm sorry you had to deal with that asshole," Derrick says. "I can't believe he would think it was okay to be out here alone with you like that." He shakes his head. "He has no sense of boundaries."

You have no idea. "Can we please go back to the hotel?" I plead.

"Of course. Do you still . . . . I mean, are we going back to the first hotel? Or the, you know, cuddle and bubble?"

"The second one."

Derrick nods, looking excited. "Okay, good. Um, not that I want to pressure you or anything."

He's not pressuring me. But now that I'm sitting here, looking at him, the boy I'm about to lose my virginity to, the boy I'm supposedly in love with, it's more clear than ever that I have to tell him the truth. Forget about whether Juliana is going to tell him. I can't sleep with Derrick unless he knows about me and Beckett.

It'll be fine, I'm sure. He'll just . . . be okay with the whole thing. I mean, it was just one kiss. How can you be upset about one kiss? And if I tell him the truth—that Beckett kissed me—then Derrick should be fine with it. Won't he? I mean, he probably won't even be thinking about Beckett once he knows we're definitely about to have sex.

"I hate that douche bag," Derrick mumbles as we walk down the street. Well, *he's* walking. I'm hobbling. My ankle is really hurting. Like, bad. I glance down at it and notice that the Band-Aid Beckett put on is starting to soak through. Great. Oh my god! I have an open wound! How am I supposed to get into a Jacuzzi that has . . . all kinds of bodily fluids in it with an open wound?

There's probably a sign on the wall that tells you to shower before you get into the Jacuzzi, but honestly, who's really going to do that? I know I wasn't planning to. What would be the point? You know everyone else isn't, so it would be a total waste of time to get yourself all clean and then hop into the gross Jacuzzi. Plus, I need my body's own bacteria to fight off the stranger bacteria that are going to be floating around in there. I picture my immune system fighting off other people's germs. My bacteria soldiers are dressed in pink, and the other ones are all gross, like little balls of gray fluff disgustingness. Like dryer lint.

Anyway. It doesn't matter, because there's no way I can get into a Jacuzzi when I have an open wound. That would just be irresponsible. No matter. I wasn't looking forward to the Jacuzzi part anyway.

We can just use the room.

"So listen," I say. "Something kind of . . . you know, weird happened earlier."

"If I see him on the street, I'm going to knock him out."

I frown. "You just saw him on the street."

Derrick looks startled, like he somehow forgot I was there. "Obviously I wasn't going to punch him in front of you," he says. "You think I would get into a fight in front of my girlfriend? Besides, I would probably end up really hurting him. And it would be disturbing for you to see that kind of anger coming from me."

"Yeah, because you're not an angry person," I say firmly.

"Yes, I am," he says. "I'm an angry person tonight. I don't like people messing with my girlfriend."

Yikes. Well then. "Okay," I say. I clear my throat and try again. "I think . . . I mean, I think we should probably maybe talk about something. I mean, I have to tell you something."

"Okay." Derrick turns around and looks at me. "What is it?" He must see the look on my face, because his eyes instantly soften. "Are you okay? What's wrong? Is it your leg?" He looks down at my leg and his eyes widen. "Oh, god," he says. "What a mess."

I look down at my ankle. A line of blood has snaked down my shin and pooled in the bottom of my shoe. A couple of girls walking by in matching sorority shirts look at me and wrinkle their noses, then keep a wide berth as they inch across the sidewalk.

"That doesn't look good," Derrick says. He bends down and gently pulls my Band-Aid off. He studies the wound. "It's not closing," he reports.

"I'm fine. I'm sure it will end up clotting once we get back to the room." Now that I've already started to tell him, I want to get this show on the road. I just want the whole thing to be over with.

Derrick stands up. "I don't think you're going to be able to get there," he says. "Every time you try to walk, you're going to break it back open."

"But when I sit down, I should be fine."

He shakes his head. "I don't think so."

"So what should I do?" I ask.

I'm not sure, but I think I see a look of annoyance pass briefly over his face. "You're going to have to go to the hospital."

"This looks like a sketchy part of town," I say half an hour later as our taxi pulls up in front of the emergency room.

"This isn't a sketchy party of town," Derrick says. He reaches into his wallet and pulls out some money and hands it to the cabbie. I'm not sure, but for a second, I think I can see him giving me an eye roll. Why would he roll his eyes at me when I'm in a weakened state?

I look out the window of the cab. Okay, I guess Derrick's right. This isn't a bad part of town, it's just a little more city-like. There were no hospitals on the island, so we had to take a taxi into the main part of Sarasota.

"Are you coming?" Derrick asks. He's standing outside the cab, the door open, looking in at me like I'm being an idiot.

"Yes." I take his outstretched hand and scooch forward on the seat, until my legs are hanging out the door. Then I stand up. There's a weird ripping sensation coming from my ankle, and I look down, expecting to see a gaping wound. But it's just my same wound, covered with a fresh Band-Aid that Derrick got for me at a drugstore while we waited for the taxi to show up. This one's starting to bleed through now, too.

"Can you walk?" Derrick asks.

"Yes." Well. I can hobble. We hobble toward the door. We hobble inside the lobby. We hobble up to the desk. We hobble over to the waiting room chairs with the forms the nurse gave us to fill out.

"They're probably going to call my mom," I say.

"So? You already spoke to her."

"I know." My mom happened to call me on my way over here. It was a relief to know that my phone was at least kind of working, even though the screen was still a complete mess. I told her I'd gotten the smallest cut ever and I was going to the doctor to get it looked at. She didn't even freak out that much, even though I texted her a pic of the wound so she could see how bad it was. It was very hard, texting on my ruined phone. I had to be careful not to get any shards of glass in my fingers.

"So then who cares?"

I shrug and fill out the forms, thankful I have my license and my insurance card in my purse.

Derrick brings everything back up to the window, then sits back down, his leg jittering nervously.

"You okay?" I ask.

"Yeah." He glances at his watch. I can tell he's annoyed we had to come here, but he's trying not to show it. Actually, he might be kind of annoyed with *me*. We got into a little bit of an argument while we were waiting for the cab. Derrick wanted to call our class adviser, Mr. Beals, and tell him what happened. I thought it was a ridiculous idea. If we called the class adviser, then we'd have to wait for someone from the school to come meet us and take us to the hospital. We'd probably have to fill out an accident report for the school's records, and then we'd be stuck going to the hospital with some stupid chaperone.

Derrick thought it was too dangerous to keep it from the teachers, like if they found out another way, we were going to get in trouble. And then I told him that if he was willing to take that chance to go to cuddle and bubble (yes, I said those words), then he should take that chance to take me to the hospital. And *then* I said if we got done at the hospital quick enough, that maybe we could still go to the hotel he'd picked out. It was actually a really annoying fight. What guy would risk having sex with his girlfriend just to tell a teacher what happened? It didn't make sense.

Whatever. It doesn't even really matter. Because looking around the waiting room, it seems like we might be here for a while. The place is packed. I start cataloging all the other patients in my head, wondering which ones might be worse off than me and therefore probably going to get called in first.

The guy in the corner, definitely. He's sitting in a wheelchair, wearing a long-sleeved plaid shirt, and he's hunched over, his head in his hands like he has a headache and can't take the pain anymore. There's a little boy in fire-truck pajamas curled up in his mom's lap. His face looks feverish, and his eyes are glazed. Definitely a child should get in before me.

"I think we're going to be here a while," I say.

"Yeah, no shit."

"You don't have to give me attitude about it," I say. "It's not my fault I got hurt."

He snorts. Well. It's a half snort. The kind of snort he's probably hoping I'm not going to hear.

"What?" I ask. "It is?"

"Well, you're the one who dropped your phone."

Good point. I wonder what he would say if he knew I actually threw it onto the pavement in a fit of rage. He would definitely think it was my fault then. "Whatever," I grumble. "You don't have to be mean to me."

"Look, I'm sorry," he says. He reaches out and takes my hand. "I'm just disappointed. This isn't how I was expecting this night to go."

"Me neither!" I say.

He looks me right in the eye, and I try not to be mad at him. I try to think about how when I first met him, he'd take me out for hamburgers after school, and I loved the way he would open my ketchup packets for me. My heart squeezes. I love him. Don't I love him? How can I love someone and then kiss someone else? Am I too young to know what love even is? That's what my mom is always telling me. Quinn used to say it, too. That love isn't just your hormones running around all crazy, that you have to have a history, a life built with someone, before you can really love them.

But then wasn't kissing Beckett just my hormones? I know it was. I don't even know Beckett. Is that why I'm too young for love? Because I can't keep myself from kissing other people?

I feel tears starting at the back of my eyes, burning, and then before I know it, one slips down my cheek.

"Hey, I'm sorry," Derrick says. "I really am. Don't cry."

I want to tell him not to be mean to me, but I don't. How can I tell him not to be mean to me after what I've done?

His fingers squeeze harder around my hand. "I'll do better. I promise."

"No." I shake my head. "I don't deserve it." All of a sudden I can feel something building inside me—it's what I was trying to let out when I smashed my phone. But it didn't work. The tension didn't go away—it just got worse. I have to tell Derrick. I have to tell him now or I'm going to explode.

My head is going to burst all over the waiting room, right in front of the kid with the fire-truck pajamas. He'll be scarred for life.

"What do you mean you don't deserve it? That's crazy. Of course you do." Derrick brushes a piece of hair off my face. "I'm sorry I said that about it being your fault you got hurt. Of course it wasn't your fault."

"No, I . . ." I take a deep breath. It's like standing on the edge of a cliff. I'm looking down at the water. I know I can't turn back. I've climbed the mountain. And I can't get down unless I jump. "Derrick, I smashed my phone."

"I know."

"No, I mean, I didn't drop it. I smashed it on the pavement. On purpose."

"You smashed your phone on *purpose*? Why?"

"Because I saw Katie Wells in the bathroom."

Derrick shakes his head. "I have no idea what you're talking about." He looks down at my wound nervously. "How much blood do you think you've lost anyway, Lyla? Maybe I should go tell the nurse."

"No. It's not . . . I'm fine. I'm trying to tell you something." God, can't he just shut up and listen for one second? "I saw Katie Wells in the bathroom. And I got really mad at her."

"Why?"

"Because she was with Beckett." My heart is beating fast,

the blood whooshing through my body. Everything feels hot, and Derrick's grip on my hand loosens.

"But why would you be mad about that?"

I don't say anything.

"Do you like Beckett?"

"No." I don't know.

"Then I don't get it."

"Derrick, he . . . Beckett kissed me."

I expect an explosion. But instead, everything settles into an eerie silence. Even the hospital noises seem to somehow fade into the background. All I can hear is the low murmur of the TV in the corner and the slow breathing of the man in the wheelchair.

It stays that way for what feels like forever.

"When?" Derrick finally asks.

"This morning, on the beach."

"This morning?" He looks stunned. "You were with me this morning."

"Before that. You were sleeping. He . . . he came to my room and told me that Quinn was—"

"You left the hotel with him?" He drops my hand. "He came to your room and you *left* with him?"

"He told me Quinn was in trouble. And that we had to go help her."

"Who gives a fuck what he told you, Lyla?" His voice is rising now, and the mother holding her son in the corner gives us an uncomfortable look. Probably she's a little nervous about her son being witness to a domestic disturbance.

"Keep your voice down," I say.

"Oh, now you're going to tell me what to do?" He takes in a long, slow, deep breath, his nostrils flaring. "So then what? He kissed you? Why didn't you tell me? I would have kicked his ass when I had the chance."

He gets up and starts to pace the floor back and forth.

"Sit down," I say.

He sits back down.

"It wasn't . . ." I swallow. "It wasn't like that." *Stop, stop, stop, stop.* There are alarms going off in my head, the kind of alarms that are telling me not to do this, to stop right this second, that something really bad is about to happen.

"Oh, yeah?" he says softly. "Then what was it like?"

Lie. Lie. Lie. The voice in my head is telling me to lie, that I should say Beckett kissed me, that Beckett is a complete asshole for doing that, that I didn't kiss him back. I'm about to ruin everything with Derrick, and for what? A stupid kiss? *Don't throw it away, don't throw it away, stop, stop, stop.*

"He . . . he kissed me and I kissed him back." Derrick stiffens next to me, but he still doesn't say anything. I feel like I'm in a nightmare, one of those ones where you're trying desperately to wake up, but you can't. For a moment, I want to take the words back, to tell him I was joking, but it's too late. I've told him the truth, and I can't change it now.

"You kissed him back?" he finally repeats.

"Yes."

"And then you got mad at him because he brought Katie to the club."

"Yes."

More silence.

"Do you like him?" he asks me again.

"No. I don't know."

He looks at me, and his eyes are filled with hurt and heartbreak, and I reach for his hand but he pulls it away. I want to throw myself at his feet and beg him to forgive me. "Don't," he says, and his voice is cold. "Just don't."

"Derrick, please, I don't . . . I don't want anything to break us up."

He makes this weird sort of sound, almost like a laugh, but it doesn't actually get there. It's like a laugh he was holding in. "Really? You don't want anything to break us up, but you kissed another guy this morning and you were going to sleep with me tonight? Were you even going to tell me before we slept together?"

"Obviously." Maybe.

He doesn't reply.

After a few seconds, I say, "It didn't mean anything." The words are hollow, even to me. And as I'm saying them, I know they're not true. It obviously did mean something. It meant a lot of things. It meant I was cheating on my boyfriend.

It meant I was attracted to Beckett. It meant I liked him enough to kiss him, to get upset at him when he brought Katie to the club. It meant everything.

"Yeah, well," Derrick says. "It meant something to me."

And then he gets up and walks out.

Well. So this is how it is. Me, sitting in a hospital waiting room, by myself, with no one. My boyfriend has broken up with me. Are we broken up? Maybe he just went for a walk. But I know it's not true. He didn't just go for a walk. He's not coming back. I told him I kissed another guy, and now that's it. Finito. Dunzo. Finale. Bye.

The woman with her son gives me a sympathetic smile.

But I don't return it. What do I have to smile about? I'm probably going to die in this hospital. I'm probably going to get an infected leg with all kinds of disgusting bacteria in it. I saw something about that on TV. How hospitals are actually the most dangerous places to be because there are all kinds of germs lurking around.

First they'll cut my leg off, and then they'll tell me I'm okay but it won't be true. The infection will have spread all through my body, and it'll start shutting my organs down one by one until it finally gets to my heart. And then it will turn my heart black, the way it obviously should be. Black, black, black. And it will serve me right. That's what you get when you cheat on your perfect boyfriend—death by black heart.

I start to cry. Silently at first, and then finally, big, racking sobs that are shaking my body. At first I think I'm crying because my heart is broken. And it is broken. But then I realize it's not broken in the way I thought it was. It's broken not because Derrick and I might not be together anymore.

It's broken because I really did think that we would be together forever. All my dreams, all my hopes, everything that was built around the two of us, is gone. And I realize that if I really did love him, I wouldn't have kissed someone else. Actually, that's not true. I do love him. But just because you love someone doesn't mean it's going to work out. In fact, it doesn't mean that at all. All it means is that you might have a chance. And honestly, a chance doesn't mean that much.

I'm crying and sniffling, and I can tell everyone in the waiting room thinks I'm crazy. They all saw what went down, me telling Derrick everything, him threatening to punch Beckett and then walking out. They think I'm one of those people—the kind of people that if you try to help them, you end up getting caught up in their craziness.

But still. You'd think one of them would at least offer me a tissue or something.

Why am I even here? Yes, my leg is still bleeding, but I'm sure it's going to stop on its own. It has to. I'm not going to bleed to death from one little tiny wound. It's, like, impossible.

I wonder if that man in the corner brought his own wheelchair, or if it belongs to the hospital. I could get them to give me one, too, and then maybe an orderly or a volunteer will push me outside and wait with me until my taxi comes. I'll probably have to sign a paper saying I'm leaving against medical advice, but who cares? Medical advice is the least of my problems right now.

I start to cry again.

And that's when Beckett walks through the door and changes everything.

THIRTEEN

IT'S SO UNEXPECTED THAT I DON'T EVEN really believe he's there at first. It's just so . . . not right, like when you see a teacher or something at the grocery store. People belong in certain places in your life, and Beckett belongs either at school or back on the island.

He doesn't belong here, at this hospital.

He's still wearing his club outfit, the black T-shirt and jeans and shiny shoes. But this time, he's not walking with that same swagger he had when he came into the club. Now he's walking with a purpose, a take-charge purpose, like he's on a mission.

He scans the waiting room until his eyes lock on mine, and then he comes over to me.

"Hi," he says.

"Hi."

He sits down next to me, not in the seat Derrick was in,

but on the other side. It feels like some kind of sick metaphor.

"What are you doing here?" I ask, wiping at my eyes with the back of my hand and hoping he won't be able to tell I've been crying.

"I came to look for you."

"How did you know I was here?"

He shrugs. "I didn't. This is the third emergency room I checked. You know there's, like, three closer hospitals than this, right?"

"This is the best-rated one in Sarasota," I tell him. "According to *U.S. News and World Report*. Derrick looked it up on his phone."

"I'll bet he did." Beckett looks around. "Where is he?"

"Who?"

"Derrick."

"Oh." I swallow and take in a shaky breath. "He left."

"He *left?*" Beckett looks at me then, and I force myself to meet his gaze. "Jesus," he says when he sees my face. He reaches out and takes my chin in his hand, cupping it gently. "Have you been crying?"

"No."

"Liar."

"Yes."

He's still looking at me, studying my face. I want to look away, but I can't. I'm falling into his eyes again, the same way

I do every time he looks at me like this, like I'm the only girl on the planet, like I'm the most important and wonderful thing in the world.

"You told him." It's a statement, not a question.

I nod.

He nods.

"Was he pissed?"

"Of course he was pissed."

"And then he just left you here?"

"He was mad," I say, not sure why I'm sticking up for him.

"So? He shouldn't have just left you here. You don't just leave someone in an emergency room." He looks around the waiting room at the array of wounded characters. "Even if it is the best hospital in Sarasota, according to *U.S. News and World Report*."

I smile.

Beckett gets up and returns a second later with a tissue and a cup of water, and watches while I blow my nose and take a drink.

"This is embarrassing," I say.

"Why?"

"Because I'm all splotchy and gross, and because this is the second time you've had to take care of me tonight."

He shrugs. "I don't mind."

I take a deep breath. "Why are you being so nice to me?"

"What do you mean?"

I want to know why he's here. Why he went to three different hospitals looking for me. Because you don't do that unless you really like someone, do you? You don't do that unless you care about someone. You don't do that unless you've been thinking about the person. And in that moment, I start to realize how much I want him to like me.

Because I don't care if I haven't known him that long, I don't care if it's just my hormones talking. I want him to like me. I like him. For whatever reason, I like him. And I want him to like me back.

"Lyla—" he starts.

"Lyla McAfee?"

I turn to see the nurse holding a clipboard and calling my name.

I go to stand up, and Beckett stands up with me. He puts his arm around my waist so that I can hold on to him while I walk.

"I'm going with you," he says.

Two stitches. I need two stitches.

Which is really kind of awful when you think about it. Two stitches is nothing. Two stitches means you have to get all injected with a painkiller and then sit there while it feels like they're tugging your skin off and then you have to tell people you got two stitches and everyone will be like, "Oh." And not even care.

At least if I had to get, like, eight stitches it would have been more of a story. Of course, if I needed eight stitches, I don't think I would have been able to walk. I probably would have been gushing blood the whole time, and the sight of it would have made me faint.

When I'm done, I pay my fifty-dollar emergency room co-pay, and then Beckett and I stand outside and wait for the cab he called to take us back to our hotel.

We don't say much.

We actually haven't said much since I asked him why he was being so nice to me. He held my hand while they stitched my ankle, keeping up a patter of jokes with the doctor, which helped distract me from what she was doing. Not that it really hurt that much—but the idea of someone sliding a needle through my skin made me queasy.

When we were back there, in the room with the doctor, it felt normal for Beckett to be there. It was like he had a role—he was helping me the way you'd help anyone who was going through something scary. But now that we're out in front of the hospital, I'm wondering again about why he came looking for me.

The cab ride back to the hotel is quiet. It's not exactly tense—more just contemplative. I think about trying to say something at least four or five times, but I'm not sure what to say, or even what I *want* to say.

When we get to our hotel, I go to pay the cabbie, but Beckett stops me.

"I got it," he says, pulling out a money clip and peeling off some bills.

"No, no," I say. "You don't have to—"

"Lyla, I got it."

After the cab pulls away, everything is silent. The moon shines down on us and the palm trees wave in the breeze, but other than that, it's quiet. It's so late now that even the partyers have gone to sleep. There are lights glowing softly in some of the hotel windows, and my body is aching for my bed. I feel like I've been wrung out and squeezed, both physically and emotionally.

"Well," I say. "Um. Thanks. For helping me."

"Do you want to go walk on the beach?" he asks.

"Now?"

"Yeah, now."

"Isn't the beach closed?"

He rolls his eyes. "How can a beach be closed?"

"I don't know."

"So?" He looks at me, and I can see the hope in his eyes. I know he wants me to go with him.

I hesitate. I'm not sure I should really be going for a walk on the beach with the guy who caused me to cheat on my boyfriend. How can I be sure that anything that I'm feeling is real? How can I be sure that I'm not just lonely, that I don't just want to be with Beckett because I'm missing Derrick?

But the thing is, I'm not missing Derrick. At least, not in the sense of how I should be missing him. In fact, the only thing I'm feeling about the Derrick situation right now is . . . relief.

Which is confusing. How can I be feeling relieved that Derrick and I broke up when up until a few hours ago I was about to lose my virginity to him? When I left to go on this trip, all I could think about was spending time with him. And now here I am, just a few days later, feeling relieved that we broke up. It makes me feel crazy, like my brain and heart have no idea what they want.

"Come on," Beckett says, and steps closer to me. He reaches out and takes my hand. "We don't have to stay long. I'll bring you back to your room soon."

Shivers run up my fingers and through my arm, even though it's not cold out. I nod and he leads me to the beach.

"We have to stop meeting like this," Beckett says once we're walking.

"What?"

He grins. "Sorry, it was a stupid joke. You know, because we were walking on the beach this morning, too?"

"Oh. Right."

I take in a deep breath of salty air, and it instantly starts to make me feel better. I take off my shoes and hold them in my hand as we walk, letting the cold water of the ocean tickle my toes. I make sure not to let any water get near my wound, but after a few minutes, my feet are hurting. We're coming upon a section of the beach that's outside one of the other hotels, and there are a bunch of comfy-looking lounge chairs lined up next to each other, facing the water.

"You wanna sit?" Beckett asks me.

I nod. We sit down on the end of one of the chairs, side by side, our knees touching. From inside my purse, my phone starts vibrating.

"I should get that," I say. "It's probably my mom."

But when I pull out my phone, it's not my mom. It's that stupid email.

Before graduation, I will . . . *learn to trust*.

I shake my head in frustration and try to exit out of the screen, but suddenly my phone makes a weird noise and then it just . . . freezes. I throw my head back and laugh. Of course. Of course that email would get stuck on my screen like that. I've done everything I could to try and get away from it, and now it's just stuck there. Probably forever.

"What's so funny?" Beckett asks. He looks down at my smashed screen. "You really shouldn't be using your phone like that. You're going to get hurt again."

I can't answer him because I'm still laughing.

"Okay," he says, and reaches over and takes the phone from me. "Why are you laughing?" I don't stop him. Maybe I should. The email's totally embarrassing, like having someone look at your freshman yearbook picture or something. (I never look good in yearbook pictures. I think it's because of my eyes. I'm always worried I'm going to blink, so I try to make sure I keep them open, and then I end up with this crazy deer-in-the-headlights kind of look in every picture.)

"'Before graduation, I will . . . learn to trust,'" Beckett recites. He shakes his head and hands my phone back to me. "I don't get it."

"It's this stupid email I wrote to myself," I say. "When I was a freshman." The water laps up against my feet, and Beckett reaches down and pulls my legs up onto the chair. "Careful," he says. "You don't want to get water in your wound."

"My wound is all bandaged up," I say, then lie back. The sky is perfectly clear, the kind of clear that doesn't happen in the Northeast. Stars sparkle down at us, and suddenly everything seems small and insignificant. Breaking up with Derrick. Hurting my ankle. Even this trip, which I was so looking forward to. I spread my arms out and take in a deep breath.

"Yeah, but you have to keep it clean," Beckett says.

"What?"

"Your wound." Beckett shakes his head. "Weren't you listening to what the doctor said?"

I giggle.

Beckett gives me a weird look. "Are you sure they didn't give you any painkillers?"

"I'm sure. It's just funny, you being the responsible one."

"Oh, yeah? Why is that funny?" He reaches behind him and grabs a lime-green pillow that's sitting on the chaise and puts it behind his head. He leans back so he's reclining in the chair, and I turn onto my side so that I'm facing him.

"I don't know. You just don't seem like the responsible type."

"How would you know what type I am?"

"Well, let's see. You ride a motorcycle, you kissed me when you knew I had a boyfriend, and now you're making me hang out with you on the beach when it's definitely closed." I tick off his infractions on my fingers.

"Fair enough." He leans his body back even more and stretches his arm out behind him. The top of his T-shirt sneaks up just a little bit, revealing a smooth strip of tanned skin that makes me feel woozy. I quickly avert my eyes. "But I'm responsible in the way it counts."

"Yeah, like what?"

"Like I'm doing a pretty good job taking care of you, aren't I?"

"Let's get through the night first," I say. "And then I'll tell you."

"Why, you think I'm going to screw it up?"

I don't say anything, just give him a smile. He shakes his head. "Ah, ye of little faith."

We sit there listening to the waves crash up against the shore. A weird feeling of peace washes over me. Which makes no sense—by all accounts, this should be the worst night of my life. I cut my leg open after smashing my phone in a fit of rage. My boyfriend dumped me in an emergency room after finding out that I cheated on him. And now I'm sitting here by the ocean with the only person who seems to care about me, and he's dangerous and bad for me and I can't stop thinking about his abs.

But there's a certain calmness that comes from hitting rock bottom. A certain kind of security in the fact that things can't get any worse. A lot of times the anticipation of bad things happening is worse than the bad things actually happening. And right now everything bad's already happened. So when you think about it, things have to get better. Right?

"So what's the deal with that email?" Beckett asks.

"I told you, it was something I sent to myself when I was fourteen."

"And you told yourself you wanted to learn to trust?"

I nod. "Yeah."

"Why?"

"Why what?"

"Why did you say you needed to learn to trust?"

I shrug. "Probably because my parents weren't really speaking to each other. And so I felt like everything was spinning out of control. I was fourteen, I had to write something. Quinn and Aven were doing it, so I went along with it, too."

"Ah." I don't like the way he's saying "Ah." He's saying it like there's more to the story, like the thought of me writing that down just because my friends were doing it doesn't make any sense. Like I have to have some deeper thought inside me, some deeper reason for writing that.

"I don't have trust issues," I say.

"I didn't say you did."

"I didn't say you said I did."

He laughs, then turns over and scoots himself down so that he's lying next to me.

"Hi," he says.

"Hi." I fall into his eyes all over again. I have a flashback to him kissing me on the beach, the way his mouth felt against mine, the way the sun brushed against my skin, his hands on my hips, his body pushed against my chest.

He reaches up and pushes my hair back from my face, then trails his fingers all the way through my hair and down to my neck. He leaves his hand there, massaging my skin gently.

His touch sends electricity through my body.

"Lyla," he murmurs.

I love the way he says my name. He makes it sound exotic and sexy and feminine. I wonder if he says Katie's name like that, but I don't care. I don't care what he's done or who he's been with or how bad he is for me. All I know is that I want to be here right now, with him, and I want him to kiss me so bad I might jump out of my skin.

But he takes his time. He strokes my hair and massages my neck and runs his fingers over my shoulders and then finally, when I feel like I'm going to explode, he puts his lips on mine. His body presses against me, and there are only two thin layers of clothes between us but it feels like too much. I rub against him and let myself get consumed by the kiss.

It goes on forever.

All night.

The two of us, kissing and looking at each other and talking.

He doesn't try to take it further, even when I'm so turned on I would have let him do whatever he wanted. Instead, he keeps me at the edge. It's so hot and sexy, like nothing I've ever thought could exist or anything I could imagine.

And finally, right before the sky starts to lighten, I fall asleep in his arms.

FOURTEEN

I'M IN THE WATER. I MUST BE. OR I'M DREAM-ing that I'm swimming. Either way, there is something wet on my cheek. I push it off.

"Go away," I mumble.

"No, I will not go away," an angry voice says.

I open one of my eyes, and the morning sunlight blinds me. There's a crick in my neck, and the side of my face feels funny. My foot is asleep, and I struggle to sit up. In the next second, it all comes rushing back to me. The club. Cutting my foot. The hospital. Breaking up with Derrick. Beckett. The beach. The kissing. Oh, god, the kissing! My lips suddenly feel swollen and raw.

I look over to where Beckett is lying next to me. He sits up slowly and blinks. He looks adorable—his hair is messy and his clothes are wrinkled and god I want to kiss him again.

"Hello!" the same angry voice says.

I shade my eyes from the sun and look up into Derrick's face. "So this is where you've been," he says. "I've been trying to call you all night."

"My phone's broken," I say. I stand up and almost fall over because of my sleeping foot.

"I thought your phone was still working." Derrick's giving me a suspicious look, like he thinks the whole phone thing is a ruse, even though he saw it all smashed up.

"It was, but then it . . . then it stopped working." It sounds lame, even to me. But then I realize I don't *owe* him anything. Yes, I kissed another guy. But he left me in an emergency room with a busted-open leg!

"How's your leg?" he asks as if he's reading my mind.

"It's fine."

"Good." Derrick looks at me and then sighs. He glances at Beckett, who's just sitting there, not saying anything. Beckett picks up a handful of sand and lets it filter through his fingers. I expected that if this moment ever happened—the two of them being in close proximity again—it would be more explosive. I expected yelling and fighting, especially since Derrick just found me out here with Beckett, sleeping together on some random lounge chairs. But it's not like that. The moment has tension, don't get me wrong—but it's more of an uncomfortableness, not the kind of tension that is going to turn into a full-blown fight.

And that's when it hits me that it's over. Like, *really* over. Me and Derrick. My heart jumps into my throat.

"Can we talk?" Derrick asks, his voice softening.

I nod, then turn to Beckett. "I'll be right back, okay?"

Beckett shrugs. "Sure."

Derrick and I walk a little ways down the beach. It seems criminal that we're about to have a serious talk on such a gorgeous day. This kind of day should be reserved for fun talks and happy memories, not breakups. We walk for a while without saying anything, and then finally, Derrick stops and picks up a rock that's sitting on the beach. He throws it into the water, and we watch as it skims over the waves before disappearing.

"Why didn't you tell me you weren't happy?" he asks. "We could have . . . I mean, we could have worked on it."

"I don't know." I swallow. Until I got here and met Beckett, I didn't *know* I wasn't happy. But if I'd been completely happy in my relationship with Derrick, then I wouldn't have been so drawn to Beckett. "I guess I didn't know I wasn't happy."

Derrick nods. He takes in a deep breath through his nose and then purses his lips and moves them to the side, the expression he always makes when he's thinking hard about something. "I need to tell you something."

"Okay." I hold my breath and brace myself.

"Juliana."

"Yeah?"

"Last night. She came over and we . . . I don't know, I guess we hooked up."

I'm about to ask if he slept with her, but I don't want to know. What does it really matter? He's not mine anymore, even though it still stings. Who he has sex with is really none of my business. "You guys . . . I mean, did you always like her?"

"I don't know. I guess we always had a little bit of a thing. I liked her when she was going out with Brock, but then I started seeing you, and . . ." He trails off.

"Is that why you kept stalling last night?"

"What do you mean?"

"You kept stalling. About sleeping with me."

He shakes his head. "I was afraid to sleep with you. I mean, yeah, it would have been amazing, and I wanted to, don't get me wrong. It was just, you. I wanted it to be perfect for you."

"Why?"

"I don't know." He shakes his head. "I guess it was like, our relationship needed to be perfect."

I nod. I kind of understand what he means. I put all this expectation on him and on us to be perfect. But at the end of the day, perfection doesn't really exist. So all you're left with is a shallow, surface-y relationship with no substance whatsoever.

Derrick reaches for my hand and my eyes fill with tears.

We stand there like that for a moment, just watching the waves.

"Friends?" he asks finally.

"Of course. Always." But even as I'm saying the words, it seems almost impossible—being friends with him. How can you turn the boy you thought you were in love with into a friend?

"I really mean it," Derrick says, like he can sense my skepticism. His eyes are serious, and the way he's looking at me makes it hard to talk. He was the first boy to ever look at me like that, the first boy to ever make me feel special, the first boy to ever really matter.

"I really mean it, too," I say honestly.

"And if he hurts you . . ." He lets the threat trail off.

"Oh, we're not . . . we're not together."

"Still." He leans down and kisses me softly on the cheek. "Take care of yourself, Lyla," he says.

"You too."

He wraps his arms around me, and I close my eyes and hold him tight. It's the last time I'll feel his body next to mine, and even though I know this is right, that it's how it's supposed to be, I don't want to let him go.

Finally, we pull back.

He gives my hand one more squeeze.

And then he walks away.

I sit down in the sand for a moment, pulling my knees

up to my chest. I pick up a rock that's sitting on the sand and throw it into the water, just like Derrick did. I watch as it falls, then lay my head over my knees, letting my hair fall around my face.

"Good-bye," I whisper softly.

And then I stand up and go back to find Beckett.

He's not there.

There's a little sign hanging on our lounge chair that says RESERVED FOR PAM, and a woman—who I can only assume is Pam—is sitting on it. She has magazines and drinks spread out all around her, and she's wearing one of those bathing suits with a skirt on the bottom. I glance around, wondering if maybe they kicked Beckett out and he's waiting for me somewhere else. But I don't see him.

I check the snack bar. I check the bathrooms. I check the sandbar, just in case he decided to go out there for a walk. I even scan a group of people who are huddled by the shoreline, looking for dolphins. Dolphin watching doesn't seem like it would be Beckett's thing, but you never know.

He left.

The words echo through my brain.

He left, he left, he left.

He must have gone back to the hotel, I tell myself. I decide to go to his room and find him.

When I get to the cobblestone walk in front of our hotel, I realize I'm walking way too fast for my injury and the shoes I'm wearing. (Stupid heels from last night. Who even invented heels, anyway? They're one of those things that mankind would just be better off without. Once you know they exist, they're so awesome that you're willing to get a clubfoot or lose a toe just to wear them. But if they hadn't been invented in the first place, everyone could just wear flats and not even know they were missing out.) I guess it's my penance for staying out all night in the same outfit I wore to go clubbing.

I look around as I walk, slowing my pace so as not to call too much attention to myself. A man wearing a striped suit walks by, and I wonder if he can tell that I'm coming home from a hookup. Well. Not really. I mean, sleeping on the beach is not really coming home from a hookup. Is it? Am I having a walk of shame? The man gives me a disapproving look and then shakes his head. Oh my god. This is my walk of shame! I'm having a walk of shame! I wonder if it still counts if I'm walking to the room of the guy I hooked up with so I can yell at him. Probably it does.

When I get to the hotel lobby, it's deserted. Hopefully everyone is out on the beach, enjoying their last day of the warm weather. Because if people from school are around to see what I'm about to do, it's definitely going to be embarrassing.

When I get to Beckett's room, I raise my hand to knock, but then I stop. What if Derrick's in there? What if Derrick came back from the beach and he's lying on his bed crying over me or something, and then I knock on the door, looking for Beckett? That would be so mean and cruel.

The longer I stand there not doing anything, the more I'm starting to think this is a bad idea. I'm about to turn around and head back to the elevator when I hear it. A girl's voice, coming from the inside of Beckett's room.

She's talking in a low, serious voice, and then I hear her laugh.

Katie.

It's unmistakable.

It's the same laugh she did last night in the bathroom, a sarcastic little laugh like she's made a joke and she's the only one who thinks it's funny.

Then I hear another voice. A male voice. A male voice I would know anywhere, because it was whispering sweet nothings into my ear last night. Okay, not sweet nothings. What is a sweet nothing anyway? I guess it's something sweet that means nothing. In that case, it is definitely applicable.

Although Beckett didn't really say anything sweet. But he was saying my name. Over and over again until I felt dizzy.

Rage fills my body. I knock on the door.

Everything inside goes silent, like they've been caught.

Ha! They *have* been caught! If he thought he could just leave me on the beach while he snuck up here with Katie, well then, he has another thing coming.

I knock again.

"Who is it?" Katie calls.

I think about lying. But who would I say it was? Besides, they know my voice. But if I tell them it's me and they don't answer the door, it would be completely embarrassing. Hmmm. Probably better to just not say anything.

Half a second later, Beckett flings open the door.

"Hi," he says, looking happy to see me for some reason.

"Well, well, well," I say. "Look what the cat dragged in." It makes no sense. Obviously. I mean, I came here. Not the other way around. If anything, I could be talking about myself being dragged in. Which is really humiliating.

"That doesn't make any sense," he says.

"Oh, it makes perfect sense." I peer past him and into the room. No sign of Derrick, thank god, but I figured as much. No way Derrick was going to be here while Beckett was with Katie. And if he was, he probably would have texted me to let me know. Because Derrick is nice. Not right for me, but nice.

Katie is sitting on the bed in the corner, a smug look on her face. She's leaning back with her legs stretched out in front of her. Her feet look small and perfect, and her toes are painted bright pink. I hate her so much.

"Hello, Lyla," Katie says. "What are you doing here?"

Beckett steps out of the room and shuts the door behind him. "Lyla," he says. "Listen, she just—"

"Stop," I say. "Just stop." I turn around and start walking back to my room. I don't even want to yell at him anymore. I just want him to be gone. But the stupid bastard starts following me.

"Lyla," he says, putting his hand on my arm. "Wait. Let me explain."

I whirl around. "Explain what? How you left me on the beach so you could be with her?"

"She came and found me," he says. "She asked if she could talk to me, so I decided to bring her back here. It's not a big deal. I was telling her that—"

"Right," I say. "And that's why you brought her to the club last night."

"What? I didn't bring her to the club last night. We ran into each other outside. I went to the club because I heard you were there, and I wanted to see you. I ran into her outside, she took my hand, she came in with me."

"And you couldn't have told her no?"

He shakes his head like he's trying to clear his thoughts. "You're right. I should have. I guess maybe some part of me wanted to make you jealous. But that's what I've been trying to tell you. I brought her here so I could tell her to leave me alone." He takes a step toward me, but I move away.

"You wanted to make me *jealous*? So you showed up with another girl? Wow, you really are an asshole."

"I said it was some part of me that maybe wanted to

make you jealous." He takes a deep breath, and his tone softens. "Look, let me go talk to her and then you and I can talk. I'll take you to breakfast, there's this really good place—"

"I'm not going anywhere with you."

"Why not?"

"Because you're an asshole." Isn't he? Suddenly, I'm not sure. The whole thing sounds like he's playing one big game with me, and it's confusing.

Beckett looks like I slapped him, and I want more than anything to take it back. I want to apologize to him, to tell him I don't think he's an asshole, that I'm just confused, that I can't stop thinking about him, that I've never felt this way about anyone before and it's messing with my mind and I'm not acting like myself.

But before I can talk, his face hardens again. "Oh, that's really mature, Lyla. Calling me an asshole? What about you?"

"What about me?" I'm shocked that he's turning the conversation back on me. What the hell have I done to him?

"You want to talk about doing the wrong thing? You hooked up with me when you had a boyfriend!"

"You kissed me!" I say. "What was I supposed to do?"

"You kissed me back," he says. He shakes his head. "Did you ever stop to think that not everything is completely black and white, Lyla? That things are complicated, that they can exist in gray areas?"

"I don't know what you're talking about," I say, trying

to sound haughty. But my voice is faltering. Is it true? Do I not know how to let things exist in gray areas? A flash of Quinn and Aven, standing on the lawn outside of school, me telling them to get the hell out of my life hits my mind. Was that another way I lived in black and white? Refusing to be friends with them, cutting them out of my life when maybe, just maybe, we could have worked it out?

Beckett reaches out and grabs my purse. He reaches into it and pulls out my phone. "This," he says. "I'm talking about this."

He holds it up, showing me the email I wrote to myself four years ago.

Before graduation, I will . . . *learn to trust.*

"What the hell does that have to do with anything?"

"It has to do with everything! You have to learn to trust people, Lyla. You said so yourself."

"I do trust people!" I say. "I trust people who are worthy of being trusted."

"Oh, like Derrick?" he asks. He throws his head back and laughs. "God, you are so naive, Lyla. What do you think Derrick was doing all day when you couldn't find him?"

"He was with his friends." I point my chin in the air, daring him to tell me different.

"Yeah, he was with his friends," Beckett says. "But Juliana was there for part of it, too, Lyla. I'll bet he didn't mention that to you, did he?"

I swallow. "That's a lie. You're lying just to hurt me."

"And why would I do that?"

"Because that's what you do, Beckett! You lie just to hurt people. Like Katie. I'm sure you're lying to her, too."

"And you're so honest, right, Lyla? You kissed me back on that beach. You kissed me and you had a boyfriend and you pretended like it didn't mean anything to you, but it did." He shakes his head. "Trusting someone doesn't mean everything's perfect, Lyla. Learning to trust means that you trust people even when they're not perfect, even when things get messed up."

"You don't know what you're talking about," I say, trying not to cry.

"You have no idea what's going on with me and Katie," he says. "Yes, I came into the club with her last night. And the only reason I hung out with her for as long as I did was because I was sad about you. I thought you'd gone back to Derrick, that I wasn't going to ever get to spend time with you again." He shakes his head. "I fucked up. That's what I do sometimes, Lyla, I fuck up. Everyone does, even you, even Derrick." He shakes his head. "But it's what you do in those moments—that's what real trust is about. You talk about the problems, you work through them."

I'm so mad I can hardly speak. How dare he stand here and talk to me about things he knows nothing about? How dare he talk about the things that I've done wrong, the

01/31/2018

Item(s) Checked Out

TITLE   Heat of the moment /
BARCODE   33029100030832
DUE DATE   **02-21-18**

TITLE   One moment in time /
BARCODE   33029100203504
DUE DATE   **02-21-18**

Thank you for visiting the library!

Sacramento Public Library

www.saclibrary.org

things that were wrong in my relationship with Derrick? He has no idea about anything I've done with Derrick, or how I feel about him, or if I trust him or not.

"How dare you stand here and judge me," I spit.

He shakes his head again, and now his face doesn't look mad or intense anymore. It just looks sad. "That's the thing, Lyla," he says. "I'm not judging you. And I wish you could see that."

We stand there, face-to-face in the hallway, and I have that sensation again, that sliding-doors-moment feeling, like the ball is poised over the net and it could go either way. That if I say the right thing, that if I let my guard down and tell him he's right, I could get what I want.

But then it passes by, and I realize just what I'm looking at.

A guy who doesn't care about me.

A guy who doesn't care about anything but himself.

"Give me my phone," I say.

He holds it out and I take it from him.

I make it back to my room before the tears start.

FIFTEEN

I LIE ON MY BED, CRYING AND FEELING SORRY for myself, for what seems like forever but is really probably only an hour. I'm crying about everything. About Derrick, about Beckett, about myself. About this dumb wasted trip that I spent so much time looking forward to. About how stupid I was to listen to anything Beckett had to say, about how wrong I could be about my feelings. I was going to have sex with Derrick! I was going to lose my virginity to a guy I ended up breaking up with. How could I have been so wrong? And if I *was* so wrong, then how can I trust myself when it comes to anything else in my life?

Was my email right? Do I really need to learn how to trust people, including myself? Was Beckett right about me? Do I only look at things in black and white?

I think back on my relationship with Derrick, wondering if there were any signs that I missed.

Of course, when we first met, I kind of thought that maybe he wasn't smart enough for me. Okay, that's not true. He was smart. He *is* smart. He gets good grades and he studies and he's responsible. It was more like . . . we didn't vibe intellectually. Like when we were talking, a lot of times I would feel like I wanted to debate or talk about something a little more in-depth, and he wouldn't really do that with me. Or when we'd watch funny movies—he'd always be laughing at the physical humor parts, the stuff with people tripping or falling all over themselves, and I'd be laughing more at the sarcastic dialogue.

One kind of humor isn't better than the other, it's just that it was a little weird that we didn't find the same things funny. Actually, not weird, just kind of . . . I don't know, disconnected.

I sigh and roll over so that I'm looking up at the ceiling. I stretch out my toes. The housekeeping team must have come this morning, because the sheets feel clean and scratchy. I hate brand-new scratchy clean sheets. I prefer my sheets slept on for a day or two, so that they're broken in. These sheets feel foreign.

My whole body feels foreign. My brain is a mess. It's like a trapeze, going back and forth and out of control. I can't stop thinking about everything in my life, about how maybe it's all been a lie.

I'm lucky that I'm still a child. Yes, seventeen is pretty

grown up, but you're really not allowed to make that many of your own choices. Can you imagine if I'd been allowed to choose a career? Or a husband? I'd probably be married to Derrick and having an affair. It really is a miracle I haven't just dropped out of school. I'm obviously completely insane. And it's making my brain race.

The door to my room opens and Aven walks in.

She glances at me, then crosses the room and throws herself down on her cot. We both just lie there for a moment, in silence. After about ten minutes or so, I'm starting to think that maybe she's fallen asleep. I'm just about to look over and check when the room door opens again and Quinn walks in.

She also throws herself down on her bed. But unlike Aven, she doesn't stay silent.

"Why are you guys just lying here?" she asks.

"I'm sad," Aven says.

"I'm wrecked," I say.

"Life's a mess," Aven says.

"I want to go home," I say.

"Me too," Quinn says. "To all of the above."

I want to ask them what's wrong, but it's like some kind of unspoken rule that I can't. It's none of my business. We're not friends anymore. And besides, the last thing I want to do is start confiding in Quinn and Aven about what happened between me and Derrick. And me and Beckett.

"You know what?" Quinn says, propping herself up on her elbow. "This is ridiculous."

"What is?" I want to add, *Us being in the same room together?* but I don't want to hurt Aven's feelings or start a fight. I've had enough fights in these past few days to last me quite a while, thank you very much.

"That we're in Florida, and we're just sitting in this room. We should be out having adventures."

"Sounds exhausting," I say.

"Sounds depressing," Aven says.

Quinn stands up and throws a pillow at me, then another one at Aven. "Get up," she says. "We're going out."

I sit up and look at her incredulously. "The three of us? Like, *together*?"

She tilts her head. "Do you have anyone else to hang out with?"

"No, but . . ." I trail off, trying to decide which is worse. Sitting here in the room feeling sorry for myself, or hanging out with Quinn and Aven. I'm surprised to find that hanging out with Quinn and Aven actually doesn't even sound bad. It sounds kind of fun. Suddenly, I miss them. I miss them so bad it hurts.

"I'm in," Aven says happily, jumping out of bed.

"Me too." I stand up, and as I do, I get a look at myself in the mirror over the desk. Wow. I look wild. My hair is all flat on one side, probably from sleeping on a lounge chair.

My clothes are wrinkled, my face is blotchy, and my eyes are bloodshot. I look like I'm about two seconds away from mugging someone and/or robbing a bank. "But can I wash my face first?"

"Of course," Quinn says.

I wash my face and brush my hair and change into a red-and-gray-patterned sundress. I slip my feet into my flip-flops and then head back out into the room.

"Okay," I say. "I'm ready." I grab my purse off the chair and slip the strap over my shoulder. I realize I've done this dozens of times—made Quinn and Aven wait for me before we go somewhere. It feels so natural, it's weird.

But then I start to wonder if this is really a good idea, if Quinn's offhand comment about us all going somewhere together is going to end up turning into some kind of horrible disaster.

Quinn and Aven and I all glance at each other nervously, and I can tell they're thinking the same thing I am. But what are we supposed to do? No one wants to be the one to call the whole thing off, the one who has to admit she's so petty she can't hang out with the other two for the day.

Because to admit that would mean you were still invested. It would mean your feelings were hurt, that they were hurt so bad you couldn't even stand for us all to be together for even a day. And that would be admitting you cared.

And the three of us have spent the past two years pretending we don't care at all.

Of course, it's a lie.

But no one wants to be the first one to break.

SIXTEEN

WHEN WE STOPPED BEING FRIENDS, IT WAS October of sophomore year, which somehow made it worse. The beginning of the school year wasn't supposed to be when you got into a huge fight with your best friends. The beginning of the school year was supposed to be when you figured out exactly how you were going to spend the next ten months, which classes were going to be hard, which teachers were going to give you a hard time, and which boys you were going to crush on.

October was not a good time for you to get into a fight with your friends. It was also not a good time for your parents to announce they were getting divorced, but that's what happened.

It was all very *not* unexpected.

I mean, I wasn't an idiot. My parents didn't fight, but they also didn't even really . . . talk. My dad had been sleeping in

the guest room for pretty much as long as I could remember.
And so when they sat me down and told me they were separat-
ing, I knew what it meant—they were getting divorced.

I wondered if they'd waited to separate until I was
almost out of the house, but I didn't want to ask. It was way
too depressing to think about my parents wasting their lives
waiting for me to be old enough to handle them getting a
divorce when I didn't even care if they got divorced in the
first place.

So I just shrugged and said it was fine. And it was. There
was no question about who I would live with—it would be
my mom. My dad and I weren't close. It wasn't like we hated
each other or anything. He wasn't a mean father. He was just
never really around. He was a surgeon, but it never felt glamorous to me, or exciting. It just felt kind of blah. He worked
long hours, but he didn't do the kind of lifesaving surgeries
you'd see on television, the kind where they wheel someone
in at three in the morning with a gunshot wound and everything descends into chaos.

He did routine things—gallbladders, appendixes, maybe
an intestinal obstruction. He worked to the point of exhaus-
tion, and even though I knew he'd always wanted to be a
doctor, I don't think he was satisfied with his life. At all.

Anyway, my parents told me not to worry, that my dad
was taking a job in New Hampshire but that he was going to
have a house there and I could visit him whenever I wanted.

That's what they said—whenever I wanted. Not anything specific, like every other weekend, or some Christmases. I said that sounded good, and then my dad went back to work and my mom and I ate dinner and then I did my homework and went to bed.

It was two in the morning when I heard it. Crying, coming from the living room. At first, I thought it was my mom. She could be emotional about things sometimes, and I figured she must be feeling bad about the divorce.

I put on my slippers and crept down the stairs. But it wasn't my mom. It was my dad. He was still in his scrubs, sitting there on the couch, the same couch where they'd told me they were getting divorced just a few hours before.

His head was in his hands and he was sobbing.

I wanted to turn around and go back upstairs—it felt weird, like I was intruding on a moment I shouldn't have been seeing. I knew there was no way my dad would have ever wanted me to see him crying like that.

But it was too late. He'd seen me.

"Hey, Lyla," he said.

"Hi." I moved awkwardly back and forth from foot to foot. "Um, are you okay?" I thought about offering him something—tea or a piece of cake—but it somehow felt wrong. How could I offer my own father tea and cake in his own house while he sat there crying on the couch? The whole scene was very weird.

"No, no, I'm fine." He looked at me then, with the saddest look in his eyes. It was actually quite shocking. I'd never thought of my dad as someone who could look that sad. Hell, I'd never thought of him as someone who could show any kind of emotion. "Lyla," he said. "I'm sorry I haven't been more of a father to you."

"It's okay," I said. "You've been a great father." It was a lie, of course—he hadn't been a great father, but really, what else was I supposed to say? You had to tell your dad he'd been good to you when he was sitting in the living room in the middle of the night crying. And it wasn't like he'd been horrible—he'd never yelled at me, never hit me, had always made sure I had food and clothes and whatever else I wanted. When it came to fathers, I knew a lot of people who were a lot worse off than I was.

"No," he said, shaking his head. "I haven't been. And now . . . now you're grown up, and I'm just . . ." He started to sob again, and I just stood there awkwardly.

"Dad," I said finally. "Seriously, please, you don't have to feel bad."

"Lyla," he said again, and this time, he looked up at me, desperate. "Come with me."

"What?"

"Come with me. To New Hampshire. Please. I can't . . . I can't be alone. I have this house, this big house, and I just . . . you should come. To live with me."

I didn't know what to say. It was a ridiculous request. Of course I wasn't going to come and live with him. I hardly knew him. And he hardly knew me. But what are you supposed to say when someone asks you something like that? So I told him I would think about it.

He went to sleep after that, and the next morning, Saturday, I told Aven what had happened.

We were eating pancakes at IHOP after hanging out at the mall, and she stopped, mid-syrup-pour.

"Are you going to go?" she asked.

"I don't know," I said. "I'm . . . thinking about it." The thing was, I *was* thinking about it. I hardly knew my dad, but my mom and I didn't have the best relationship either. It seemed . . . I don't know, like an opportunity. I'd just broken up with a guy—this loser named Marco Price who made out with me and then pretended it never happened, which, in my deluded tenth-grade brain, felt like a breakup and not what it really was—a blow-off—and I felt like I needed to get away from things.

"Please don't tell anyone about this," I said.

"Of course not."

But she did tell someone. She told Quinn.

Aven said she thought when I said not to tell anyone, Quinn wasn't included. But she was. Because Quinn's mom was friends with my mom. And Quinn told her mom. And Quinn's mom told my mom that she was sorry to hear

I was moving to New Hampshire with my dad.

And my mom freaked out on me.

She started crying and screaming, and begging me not to go. I told her I wouldn't. But I was mad. Mad at Quinn for telling her mom, mad at Aven for telling Quinn.

Of course, neither one of them had any idea I was upset. I blew off all their texts and calls for the whole day because I didn't trust myself to talk to them.

Looking back, that was a mistake.

When I got to school on Monday morning, they were waiting for me outside.

"Yo," Aven said. "Where you been?"

"Yeah, we were trying to get in touch with you all day yesterday." Quinn was texting on her phone, and when she looked up, she must have seen the look on my face. "What's wrong? What happened?"

My plan had been to play it cool. To greet them with a calm indifference and then go from there.

But instead, I exploded.

"How could you tell her?' I yelled at Aven. "I told you not to tell anybody!"

"What?" She frowned and looked confused.

"You told Quinn! What I told you about my dad."

"Lyla, I didn't think you meant Quinn! All three of us tell each other everything." But I could see the look of doubt that was crossing her face, the slight tiny bit of guilt that let me know that she knew, at least on some level, that what she'd done was wrong.

"Wait, just calm down," Quinn said. "Lyla—"

But it was too late. I had spent all weekend being calm, but it turned out it was just a facade. I was like a serial killer who had spent the weekend in waiting, acting detached before unleashing a torrent of hurt on people. I'd thought I was taking time to figure out how I felt—but really I was just letting things simmer until I was ready to boil.

"You," I said, turning to Quinn. "How could you have told your mom?"

She got that same look on her face, the same look Aven had just gotten. "How did you know that?"

"I know that because she told my mom! And now my mom is freaking out!" I was yelling at the both of them now, loud enough that a couple of people were starting to notice. If I pushed it much further, a teacher was probably going to come outside and break it up. I almost wanted that to happen, I almost wanted a bunch of people to stare at us and for us to make a scene. I wanted the two of them to have something happen to them for what they'd done, and getting in trouble at school seemed as good of a punishment as anything.

"You told your mom?" Aven asked, turning to Quinn. "Why the hell would you do that? Your mom has the biggest mouth in the world."

"She does not," Quinn said, putting her chin in the air. "And I had no idea she was going to tell your mom."

"Neither one of you can keep a secret!" I screamed. "You realize now that both my parents hate me, right?" It was an exaggeration, of course. Neither one of them hated me. My mom had been upset, yeah, but I'd told her that I'd just said that to make my dad feel better, that Quinn and Aven must have gotten the story wrong.

I hadn't said anything to my dad, because he hadn't brought it up since the night we talked in the living room.

"Look," Aven said. "We all need to calm down."

The bell rang, signaling the beginning of first period, and we all looked at each other. "We can talk about this at lunch," she said. "We'll blow off afternoon classes. Unless . . ." She took in a deep breath. "Unless you want to go somewhere now?"

Quinn looked at me and nodded. "I'm in." It was a huge thing for her to want to skip class, which showed me how much she wanted to talk and work this out. Quinn hated doing things that were against the rules.

I wavered. For a moment, I wanted to talk to them. I needed them. They'd been the only thing that had ever been constant in my life. With my parents, everything seemed so . . . fragile, like it could be torn in half at any moment. And obviously I'd been right about that, since they'd been so glib about their divorce.

But I was too hurt. I didn't want to sit down and talk to Aven and Quinn and have them explain the ways they'd disappointed me. So instead I shook my head. "I don't want to go," I said. I was about to add "maybe later" but instead I said, "Stay out of my life."

And then I walked into school.

Later, when I got a group text asking if I would talk to them that afternoon, I ignored it. I just wanted to forget about both of them, to pretend like nothing had happened. They called and texted for a while after that. But I just ignored them. I knew, on some level, that I was isolating myself because of my parents' divorce. I just didn't want to deal with it. I thought that eventually I'd respond to one of their texts, that we'd make up, that everything would go back to the way it was. I thought I'd end up forgiving them. But by the time I was ready, they'd stopped trying. And I didn't know how to make it better.

We come up with two rules for the day.

No talking about our fight. We all agree that the last thing we want to do is start rehashing everything that happened between us. No personal questions.

No talking about the emails we sent.

"This might be awkward," I warn them as we step out onto the sidewalk in front of the hotel.

"Not any more awkward than sleeping in the same room," Quinn says.

"True."

We spend the first part of the morning walking on the beach, collecting shells until our pockets are overflowing. Then we stroll along Ocean Boulevard in Siesta Key, stopping at the farmers' market and buying gorgeous light-blue wide-mouthed glass bottles, which we pour our shells into.

"This reminds me of how we always used to buy the same things," Aven says as she corks her bottle. She holds it up to the light, letting the sun glint off the glass.

"We're not supposed to be talking about the past," I say, but there's a lump in my throat. I do remember when we all used to buy the same things. We weren't the kind of friends who didn't want anyone else to have what we had. We liked being the same.

"You wanna get lunch?" Quinn asks, ignoring Aven's remark.

"Sure."

We head to an outdoor restaurant. Everything on the menu looks amazing, so we order a bunch of appetizers to share.

"No sour cream on the fish tacos," Quinn says when we order, glancing at me. "Right?"

I nod. I don't like sour cream. And I'm glad she remembered.

"Can you believe this?" Aven asks, as we sip our frozen virgin strawberry daiquiris. "Did you ever think we'd end up sitting here together at the end of this trip?"

"No," Quinn and I say honestly.

Aven takes a deep breath. "I know we're not supposed to be talking about the past, and you don't have to give me any details, but . . . did you guys do what your emails said to do?"

I open my mouth to protest, to tell her we're not supposed to be talking about that stuff, that we *shouldn't* be talking about it. First of all, we made a rule, and second of all, it's a slippery slope. If we start talking about one thing, we're going to start talking about everything.

But then I figure, why the hell not? Let Aven ask me all the questions she wants. Do I really have anything to hide? "Yes," I say, looking directly at Quinn, daring her to stop me from answering. "Did you guys?"

"Yes," Quinn says, raising her chin in defiance.

"Yes," Aven says.

I wait for them to elaborate, to tell me what happened, but they don't. Even Aven keeps quiet.

When we finally start talking again, we make stilted small talk. But slowly, things start to loosen up, and by the end of the meal we're laughing and joking, gossiping about our classmates, talking about celebrity fashion, and debating whether Quinn should cut her hair.

It's not until we're working our way through a melting cookie-dough sundae that Quinn says, "We should do it again."

"Do what again?"

"We should make more promises. Why not? We're at the beach."

It's such a weird request, coming from Quinn, that I almost laugh. She has to be joking. But her tone doesn't sound joking. In fact, it sounds kind of shy. And tentative, like she's afraid we're going to say no.

"Sure," I say, shrugging like it's no big deal. "I'm in."

"Me too," Aven says.

We decide to skip the emails this time and go old-school, writing down our promises and making sure we get to work on them right away, instead of waiting four years. We buy paper, purple markers, and a lighter from a souvenir shop, then stand on the beach, each writing down one sentence.

I promise to . . .

I think about it.

I'm 0-for-1 when it comes to promises to myself. But maybe that's because I set myself up to fail. Learning to trust is a big thing to promise yourself, especially when you didn't even realize how deep your trust issues went. And even then, I'd given myself four years to do it.

So I take the piece of paper and write . . .

I promise to . . . learn to be happy.

When we're all done writing, we fold the pieces of paper in half.

"Ready?" Quinn asks, holding out the lighter.

I glance at Aven, wondering if she's going to ask us to all read them out loud. But even she knows that would be pushing it too far. We're not friends anymore. And even though we might have spent a few nice hours together, it doesn't mean we have the right to know what the others are thinking.

We watch as the papers flame and separate before burning out in the sand. The ashes mix with the ocean, then wash away into the sea.

The three of us sit down in the sand, not saying much, just watching the sun go down.

I promise to . . . learn to be happy.

There won't be an email this time to remind me. I'm going to have to remind myself.

We stay on the beach until the stars start to peek through the dark cloth of the night sky. And then we stand up and head back to the hotel.

SEVENTEEN

THE NEXT MORNING, WHATEVER KIND OF peace was made between Quinn, Aven, and me is gone. It's like waking up from a drunken night where you've slept with someone and then you look over and realize what you've done and decide you must have been crazy.

(Not that I've ever had any drunken nights with anyone. But I've seen enough movies to know how it works.)

When I wake up, Quinn is standing by the dresser, fully ready for the day.

"Did either one of you take my hair straightener?" she asks, looking at us accusingly.

Aven's sitting on the side of her bed, in a T-shirt and a pair of cotton shorts, blinking sleepily while she checks her phone. "I didn't," she says.

"Because it's missing," Quinn says. "And since I haven't used it, it had to have been one of you."

I rack my brain, trying to remember what happened to the straightener I used the other night. "I think it might be in the cabinet under the sink," I say.

Quinn sighs, like it's the biggest offense ever, then marches into the bathroom and retrieves her straightener.

She places it in her suitcase, then turns to us. "You guys better hurry up. You're going to be late." She wheels her suitcase through the door and out into the hallway.

I sigh and glance at the clock. Our class is meeting down in the lobby so that we can take the bus back to the airport. We're supposed to be down there in twenty minutes.

"Do you mind if I shower first?" Aven asks. "I won't take long."

"No, I don't mind," I say, deciding to just skip my shower. Why get all clean when I'm just going to end up on a disgusting airplane anyway? "Just let me wash up real quick." I head to the bathroom, pee, wash my face, brush my teeth, and pull my hair back into a ponytail. Then I throw on a pair of yoga pants, a tank top, and a hoodie.

When I'm done, Aven's waiting outside the bathroom door, holding a container of body wash and a bottle of shampoo.

"See you down there," I say awkwardly as she passes me by.

When I finally get down to the lobby, it's a madhouse. Kids are all over the place, running around, talking, joking, and carrying on. I head to the corner and pour myself a cup of coffee from the carafe on the table. Usually I hate the taste of coffee, but I feel like I need something to do, something to concentrate on.

I spot Derrick in the corner, talking to Juliana. I watch them for a moment, at the way she's laughing at something he's saying. I think about how he was with her the other day when he just disappeared. I think about how he was talking on the phone when I came to his room, how he told me he was talking to his mom.

Was he really talking to Juliana? I'm surprised to find that I don't really care. Derrick isn't mine anymore. He's not my boyfriend. And if he was talking to other girls while we were together this weekend, well, then, I really have no right to be mad. I was kissing another guy.

I take my coffee and head outside, waiting on the bench in front of the hotel until it's time to get on the buses. I concentrate on my coffee as we board, making sure to keep my eyes down. I don't want to see Derrick with Juliana, but most of all, I don't want to see Beckett. I don't want to know if he's on the same bus as me, I don't want to know if he's with Katie, I don't want to know anything about him.

I repeat the whole process at the airport, and on the flight, making sure to always have a drink or a snack to concentrate on, always making sure to keep my eyes on the ground. All I want to do is get home. Traveling under any circumstances is extremely tiring, but this feels like a marathon. Bus to the airport. Flight back to the Northeast. Bus to school. And then waiting for my mom to come and pick me up.

I texted her earlier to confirm the time, but when our bus is finally pulling into the school, she texts me back to tell me she got held up at meditative yoga, and she's going to be a little late.

Everyone else is happy and chatty and sunburned. They're all hugging their parents and telling them all about the trip, and I'm just standing there feeling sorry for myself. I head to the back of the bus, where our suitcases have been unloaded onto the sidewalk.

But when I get there, Beckett's standing by my suitcase.

"Oh," he says, like he's surprised to see me. "I was going to . . . I mean, I was going to bring this to you."

"Thanks," I say, "but I can handle it." I grab the handle and start to roll it away, down the pavement and back toward the craziness of the traffic circle.

"Lyla," Beckett calls.

I have another one of those moments—the kind where things are about to go one way or the other, and I feel if I don't make the right choice, I could mess everything up. I could keep walking, leaving Beckett behind. Or I could turn around and listen to what he has to say. But why would I do that? Beckett's a jerk. He told me himself that he doesn't like to have expectations put on him. When someone tells you who they are, you need to believe them. I heard it from Oprah, who heard it from Maya Angelou. Why would I want to set myself up for more of that torture? I feel horrible enough already.

Before graduation, I will . . . learn to trust.

But isn't knowing who to trust part of trusting? Beckett has proven to me that he can't be trusted. He showed up with Katie right after kissing me. *Oh, come on. He hasn't done anything worse than you did, and you know it. You had a boyfriend and you kissed Beckett anyway and then you blew him off and blamed everything on him. Just like he said. In fact, you're kind of being a spoiled brat, using any excuse to get mad at him because you're afraid.*

I turn around.

"Fine. Say what you want to say."

EIGHTEEN

WHEN I WROTE IT—THE EMAIL TO MYSELF—IT
had nothing to do with my dad. It was one of the first days
of high school, more than a year before my parents were
even going to tell me they were getting divorced. (Not that
I thought their marriage was that great—I knew my parents
didn't sleep in the same bed, and I knew my dad worked
way too many hours for it to be possible for him to have a
healthy marriage.)

Anyway, my dad was the last thing on my mind when I
wrote that email. It was right at the beginning of freshman
year, right after Evan Winters kissed me at a back-to-school
party and told me I was the prettiest girl in the whole school,
which was obviously a lie but I didn't care. The next day,
he completely blew me off, cruising by me in the halls and
acting like nothing had ever happened. Fourteen-year-old
me, who didn't know any better, was devastated. I didn't

understand how Evan could do that, and honestly, the whole high school thing was starting to feel like a big rip-off. Aven, Quinn, and I were extremely disappointed by how it was going. We'd thought high school was where we'd make our mark, where we'd finally have a chance to *do* something.

But it was the opposite—the school felt big and overwhelming, and all the kids seemed more cliquey than ever, and the guys were obviously jerks.

We decided it was going to be up to us to make sure we made our mark. So we went to the beach the next weekend and decided to come up with goals we wanted to accomplish before graduation, write them in an email, and send them to be delivered four years in the future.

I wrote that I wanted to learn to trust. At the time, I remember it being all about Evan. I had no idea what was about to happen with my dad. I didn't know that my dad was going to leave, that he was never going to mention the fact that he'd asked me to come with him, that he'd pretty much ignore me after he left.

The only thing I had left that connected me to him was my tigereye bracelet. He'd given it to me a couple of months before he left—he told me that whenever I was feeling upset or down, to remember I had the eye of the tiger. At first, I was confused. I wasn't going through a particularly hard time at that point. But then my dad reminded me that when I was little I used to love that song, that we used to blast it in his truck whenever we drove anywhere together.

I had vague memories of that, but it wasn't, like, our thing. At the time I remember thinking he was just being a normal parent, idealizing the things we'd done together when I was younger, like when my mom bought me a DVD copy of *Follow That Bird* for Christmas one year, and then told me I used to love watching it when I was three.

I put the bracelet in my jewelry box and forgot about it. But now I think maybe my dad knew he was eventually going to leave. It was his way of giving me some kind of parting advice before he was gone forever. The day Quinn and Aven and I got into that fight, I went home and slipped the bracelet on. I haven't taken it off since.

These are the things I'm thinking about while I wait for Beckett to tell me why he called my name, why it is that he stopped me.

He's certainly taking his time.

The problem is that there are still cars pulling up to the school—parents arriving to take their kids home from the trip. The traffic circle is filled with cars, and now the line is snaking farther down, more toward where Beckett and I are, making privacy impossible.

I'm sitting on the curb, and he's sitting next to me. My suitcase is on the other side of me, and I'm gripping the handle protectively. If I decide to take off in a hurry, I'm ready. Finally, after most of the cars have cleared out, and the only people left are some stragglers way up by the front door, Beckett speaks.

"I owe you an apology."

"For?"

"Actually, not really an apology. More of an explanation."

I wait, but he doesn't say anything. "Go ahead," I say. "I'm listening."

"I need to explain to you about Katie," he says after another beat of silence. He takes in a deep breath and reaches down and fiddles with his shoelace. It's the first time I've ever seen him do something that even remotely made it seem like he was nervous. Is Beckett anxious? About talking to me?

"Katie and I . . . I'm sorry I brought her into the club with me. I knew you were going to be there, and when I saw you with Derrick, I don't know . . . I guess I was *hoping* it might hurt you a little bit to see me show up with another girl."

I still don't say anything.

"After I kissed you on the beach, and you . . . you just . . . came to my room and were looking for Derrick, I kind of freaked out."

"You freaked out? Why?"

"Because I like you, Lyla." He fiddles with his shoelace some more, and then he turns to look at me. "You're interesting and gorgeous and smart and you don't put up with any of my shit. It's why I came to your room to tell you about

Quinn, even though I pretty much knew she was okay." He shakes his head. "I was trying to make you jealous with Katie. It was a horrible, shitty thing to do and I'm sorry. I just . . . I really felt like maybe if you saw me with someone else, you might decide you wanted to be with me. But it was a stupid idea, and I shouldn't have used Katie like that."

"Did you apologize to her, too?"

He nods. "That's what I was doing when you found her in my room yesterday. I wanted to apologize to her for the way I'd treated her, and tell her that I wanted to be with you. I'd already told her we kissed, that I liked you, but I guess she didn't quite believe me."

My first instinct is to tell him he's a shithead. "What you did wasn't right," I say instead.

He nods. "I deserve that." He's been moving closer to me on the curb as we've been sitting there, so slowly that I don't even notice until his leg is pressed up against mine. "But don't I get points for being honest?"

I shake my head no. "I can't . . . I mean, how could I ever trust you?"

He tilts his head like he's actually thinking about it. Then he reaches out and takes my head. His palm is warm and comforting, and I don't pull away. "Trust has to be earned, that's true," he says. "But do you think . . . I mean, could you give me a chance?"

Before graduation, I will . . . learn to trust.

I think about the stuff Beckett said about how I only see things in black and white. Is it true? Do I see things in just one shade, either good or bad? And if so, is that really the way I want to live my life?

I think about that email, about how it kept appearing this weekend, about how it's now stuck on my phone. Do I really know how to trust? Or was it just that Derrick didn't really make me have to learn? Everything with him was so . . . easy. We never had to work through things, we never even had a real fight. Was I with him just because he didn't challenge me, because he didn't make me see things in another way? Looking back, our relationship seems so surface-y. I feel like Beckett and I have gone through more in a few days than Derrick and I did in a couple of years.

"Lyla," Beckett says again. I turn to look at him, and his face is just a few inches from mine. "Please, I . . . I'm not going to hurt you. I promise." I can tell that he means it. I can see the sincerity on his face, hear the vulnerability in his voice. I can sense he's never been this real with a girl before, never really put himself out there in this way.

"I don't know," I say, pretending to think about it. "I mean, what is everyone at school going to think?"

"They're probably going to be shocked that I've turned into some kind of lovesick puppy."

"What are they going to think about me?"

He leans even closer and then breathes into my ear. "I

don't care what they think. All I care about is what I think.
And I think you're perfect."

And then he kisses me, and the moment fades away into
everything I could ever imagine.

I call my mom and tell her that I'm getting a ride home. Of
course, I don't mention who it's with. Thank god she doesn't
ask questions—when she answers the phone, her voice is all
whispery, like she's still at her yoga class and doesn't want
other people overhearing. She probably assumes Derrick's
taking me home, and she's probably relieved she doesn't
have to come and get me.

Beckett drove his motorcycle to the school from the
airport, but my suitcase won't fit on the back—so he kisses
me one more time and takes off for his house, where he's
going to drop his motorcycle off and then return in his dad's
car—a Dodge Durango, which seems a lot safer.

Even though the sun is starting to go down, it's warmer
than I would expect it to be this late in the afternoon. Spring
is coming. You can feel it in the air. The days are getting longer and warmer, and there are only a couple of months of
school left.

And then I'll be off to college. What will happen with
me and Beckett? Whatever. I can't really worry about that.
That's months away, and besides—I have to trust myself

that I'll figure it out. That *we'll* figure it out.

I don't even realize that I'm humming a little tune to myself until I'm standing in front of the school and one of the few kids who's still waiting outside gives me a weird look.

"Sorry," I say. "I'm just really happy."

My phone beeps with a text, and I pull it out of my pocket.

Hey, it's Aven—I'm locked in the bathroom by the gym, can you please come and—

The rest of her text is blocked out by the email that's frozen on my screen.

I sigh. Why is Aven texting me if she's locked in the bathroom? Doesn't she have any other friends to call? And how did she lock herself in the bathroom anyway? And how does she know I'm still even here?

I'm tempted to just ignore it. But what if she's in real trouble? What if she's locked in the bathroom and she can't get out? Well. She'd get out tomorrow morning. We have school, and someone would find her.

But do I really feel okay just leaving her there overnight? How humiliating. And besides, what if there's a fire or something?

I sigh and haul my whole suitcase into the school with me. When I get to the bathroom by the girls' gym, Quinn is there.

"Hey," she says.

"Hi." I frown. "Are you . . . did Aven send you a text, too?"

"Yeah, about being locked in the bathroom?"

We both look at each other in confusion. I shrug.

"Whatever," Quinn says, then pushes open the door.

I follow her inside, but the bathroom is empty.

"Aven?" I try. I have a vision of her drowned in one of the toilets, unable to come up for air. I'm not sure exactly how that would happen. But still.

I start pushing open stall doors, and Quinn follows suit.

But before we can get to every stall, the door to the bathroom opens and Aven comes sauntering in.

"Aven!" Quinn says. "Why the hell did you tell us you were locked in the bathroom?"

"Yeah," I say. "I was worried about you."

But Aven doesn't answer us. She just turns around, and then calmly locks the door behind her.

"What the hell are you doing?" Quinn demands. She walks to the door, but Aven just smiles and puts the key back in her pocket. How the hell does Aven have a key to the bathroom anyway?

"I'm sick of this," Aven says. "I'm sick of not being friends. I'm ready to make up." She takes in a deep breath and looks at us, determined. "And none of us are leaving this bathroom until we do."

THE NEXT STORY IS QUINN'S—
READ ON FOR A SNEAK PEEK!

LAUREN BARNHOLDT

Author of *Two-way Street*

ONE
MOMENT
IN
TIME

THE MOMENT OF TRUTH BOOK 2

HE TURNS TO ME. "DO YOU WANT TO GET OUT of here?"

"What?"

"Do you want to leave?"

"With you?"

"Yes, with me."

"I can't *leave* with you," I say. "I just met you, like, five seconds ago." I mean, how stupid could I be? Leaving a club with some guy I know nothing about? That's insane. It's how people end up disappearing and/or chopped up into a million pieces, just like my brother said.

"Five hours."

"What?"

"We met five hours ago. On the beach."

"I can't just leave with you," I say again. "I don't know anything about you."

"You know my name. And where I work."

"But that's all."

"True," he says seriously. He cocks his head and pretends to think about it. "Actually, I think you're right. It wouldn't really make sense for us to hang out. Since I'm a stranger and everything."

"It *wouldn't* make sense," I say. "It wouldn't be *smart*." I resist the urge to list all the reasons it's a bad idea, because I don't want to insult him by implying he could be a psycho murderer. Besides, it's really not something that needs to be explained. Is he used to girls just going home with him? He doesn't seem surprised I don't want to leave with him. But he doesn't seem particularly upset about it, either. Does he figure that if I turn him down he'll just find someone else to take home? I'm vaguely repulsed, but also slightly excited, like I'm going to miss my chance. Which is awful and against any kind of feminism, like, ever.

And then I remember that stupid email.

Before graduation, I promise to . . . *do something crazy*.

Yes, something crazy. But not something *dangerous*. Something dangerous like going home with a guy I just met. Something dangerous like going home with a guy I just met while on vacation in a strange place. He's cute, yes. And he seems harmless enough, albeit cocky. But still . . .

Don't overanalyze it. How are you feeling—what do you want to do?

I take in a deep breath.

And then, before I can change my mind, I turn and look at him.

"Okay," I say. "Let's get out of here."

THREE GIRLS.
THREE STORIES.
ONE UNFORGETTABLE TRIP.

Don't miss the complete **MOMENT OF TRUTH** series by Lauren Barnholdt.